Lucy
and the
WOLF IN SHEEP'S CLOTHING

Lucy
and the
WOLF IN SHEEP'S CLOTHING

ANN JUNGMAN

Illustrated by Karin Littlewood

Collins

An imprint of HarperCollinsPublishers

In memory of Tristan Wood –
who liked to laugh

First published in Great Britain by Dragon Books in 1987
Published in Young Lions in 1989
This edition published by Collins in 1998
Collins is an imprint of HarperCollins*Publishers* Ltd
77-85 Fulham Palace Road, Hammersmith, London, W6 8JB

1 3 5 7 9 8 6 4 2

Text copyright © Ann Jungman 1987
Illustrations copyright © Karin Littlewood 1987

ISBN 0 00 673271 2

The author and illustrator assert the moral right to be
identified as the author and illustrator of the work.

Printed and bound in Great Britain by Caledonian International
Book Manufacturing Ltd, Glasgow G64

Chapter One
DOWN ON THE FARM

One winter morning Lucy Jones put on her warm boots, her thick woolly tights and her bright red anorak and set off down the forest path to go to school. The last time she had walked in the forest dressed in her anorak a wolf had mistaken her for Red Riding Hood and her adventures with 2.15 had begun.

"Still, that's all ancient history now," Lucy thought as she hurried briskly through the woods, for she did not want to be late. Then she heard a rustling in the undergrowth near the path – she was being followed.

"2.15," Lucy called. "Is that you?"

"It most certainly is, dear one," replied the wolf, coming out of the shadows. "But you shouldn't have guessed. You spoiled my fun! I was going to leap out and say, 'I am your dinner and you are my destiny' – no, no, no I got it all wrong!" he cried.

"I am your destiny and you are my dinner," they said together.

"Well, I'm sorry if I spoiled it," said Lucy, "but I'm in a hurry."

"Why?" asked 2.15.

"Because I'm going to school," explained Lucy.

"Oh, is that all?" said the wolf cheerfully. "Oh well, then you've got plenty of time to chat to me."

"No, I haven't, 2.15. Now what do you want?"

"I want to know when your gran and grandad are moving down here to the forest," the wolf said. He was a great friend of Lucy's grandparents and had helped them get enough money to buy a little cottage in the forest.

"Just after Christmas," replied Lucy. "Why?"

"Well," responded the wolf, "I think that they may need some help packing up and so on. After all, moving is a big event."

"I know," agreed Lucy. "I'm going to London to give them a hand when term finishes."

"Oh good," said 2.15 approvingly. "Then you can take me along with you so they can have the advantage of an extra pair of paws."

"Oh no, 2.15," groaned Lucy.

"Why do you say 'Oh no', dear girl, after all the fun we had together last time we went to London?"

"But I thought you and your wife, 3.45, were busy living happily ever after here in the forest," said Lucy.

"Oh, we are. Oh yes indeed, very happily. But you know how it is,

How are you going to keep 'em down on the farm
Now that they've seen Paree?" sang the wolf.

"Whatever are you on about?" groaned Lucy. "I've never been able to understand half of what you say."

"Oh dear, oh dear, oh dear," said the wolf. "What you children learn at school I shall never know. Now, you sit down on that tree trunk and I will perform the piece for you correctly."

Lucy sighed and sat down, knowing that it was now certain that she would be late for school. A moment later 2.15 emerged from behind a tree wearing a boater and with a cane under his arm. He kicked his legs up in the air as he sang with a broad American accent:

*"How're you going to keep 'em down on the farm
Now that they've seen Paree?"*

and as soon as the song was finished, he knelt down with his arms outstretched towards Lucy.

"Now do you understand?"

"No," said Lucy, "not at all."

"Paree is Paris – you know, the capital of France? Well, once people have seen a big city like that, they don't want to just hang around in the country. Now do you see?"

Lucy shook her head.

"I shall have to spell it out for you. I am languishing for the big city. I want you to take me on the 2.15 to London just one more time, for a little saunter down memory lane, so that I can meander among my memories, nestle in nostalgia and ramble among my reminiscences."

"Hmmmmm," said Lucy, and then she looked at her watch. "Oh no," she cried. "I'm going to be terribly late," and she ran off, leaving 2.15 to his own devices.

When school finished Lucy walked back home thinking about 2.15. She heard a rustling in the undergrowth and then found herself looking straight into the eyes of a wolf.

"Oh, 2.15, go away. I have to think about it, and you're not to pester me while I do," she cried.

"It's not 2.15," said the wolf in a sharp tone. "It's 3.45."

3.45 was the lady wolf 2.15 had rescued from the zoo on his first trip to London. Lucy hadn't seen her since they had come back to the forest.

"3.45," said Lucy, amazed. "I didn't know you could speak English."

"Why shouldn't I be able to?" snapped the wolf. "Do you think I'm stupid or something?"

"Oh no," said Lucy quickly. "But I thought that as you were a real wolf you wouldn't be able to talk."

"'Course I can talk," snorted 3.45. "Learnt since I've been in the forest. Himself taught me."

"Oh," said Lucy, who was still a bit stunned by the surprising revelation that 3.45 could also talk.

"What I want to know," said 3.45, "is what my crazy husband asked you to do this morning?"

"Well, honestly, 3.45," said Lucy, "I'm sure he'll tell you himself."

"I'm just as sure that he won't. Come on – either you tell me, or I'll take a nip out of your knees!"

"Oh dear," sighed Lucy. "I don't know what to do."

3.45 growled and snapped her teeth.

"Oh, all right," groaned Lucy. "He wants me to take him to London."

"Huh!" said 3.45. "I thought as much. And he plans to leave me here on my own, I suppose?"

"It would only be for a little while. He said you and he were very busy living happily ever after, but he felt like a change, and he wants to help Gran and Grandad move and see to it that they live happily ever after, too."

"He's crazy, that one," announced 3.45. "All he thinks about is that people should live happily ever after."

"Don't you want people to live happily ever after, then?" asked Lucy.

"Not me," said 3.45. "I'm not that keen on people – I think people are a waste of time, a complete waste of time."

"Oh, come on!" said Lucy. "You don't really think that."

"Jolly well do," insisted the wolf. "And if you'd ever been in a zoo you'd think so too. All those people gawping at you and saying silly things – how would *you* like it?"

"Umm," replied Lucy. "I'd never thought of it like that. I suppose you're right."

"Jolly well am," said 3.45. "And you ought not to help 2.15 go to London. You ought to help me keep him here – us girls ought to stick together."

"I suppose so," answered Lucy. "But I don't think of you as a girl."

"Well, I am," said 3.45, "and you should be helping me, not him."

"It's very hard, 3.45," explained Lucy. "After all, I've known him so much longer than I've known you."

"Good afternoon, ladies," came a voice, and there, standing in front of them, leaning against a tree and smiling broadly, was 2.15. "What a joy and delight to see my two favourite ladies strolling together through the leafy forest glades."

"2.15," said Lucy sternly, "you didn't even talk to 3.45 before you asked me to take you to London."

"Well, of course not, my love," replied 2.15 smoothly. "Naturally I didn't want to worry her until it was a reality."

"She says she doesn't want you to go," said Lucy.

"Of course she doesn't," said 2.15. "She doesn't like the idea of a few days on her own without her own true love, do you, dearest?"

"I don't mind a few days on my own one bit!" snapped 3.45. "What I don't want is you going to town and getting into all sorts of trouble without me to keep an eye on you."

"If 3.45 doesn't want you to go, then I won't take you," pronounced Lucy. "And that's final."

"All right," said 2.15 amicably. "If you two ladies wish me to remain in the forest, who am I to argue? So be it."

Feeling a bit uncomfortable by the ease with which 2.15 had given in, Lucy left the two wolves and went home. Over tea, she told her mother about her misgivings.

"3.45 just wouldn't allow him to go to London," Lucy said, "so 2.15 had to give in."

"That doesn't sound like 2.15," commented her mother. "I expect he's planning something at this very moment."

For a few days nothing happened, and Lucy began to believe that her mother's prediction had been wrong. Then one morning there was a knock at the door and in came their next-door neighbour, Pete Grubb. Lucy always felt a bit anxious when she saw Pete Grubb. She remembered only too well how 2.15 had tricked and deceived him during the wolf's visit to London.

"Hello, Pete," said Lucy's mum. "Come on in."

So Pete Grubb came in and sat at the kitchen table, staring gloomily into space.

"What's up, Pete?" asked Lucy's mum.

"What's up is that wolf," groaned Pete Grubb.

"2.15?" said Lucy. "Why, what's he been up to?"

"He's been watching my telly, that's what,"

said Pete Grubb, looking more sour than ever.

"Well, that doesn't sound too bad," said Lucy's mum with relief in her voice. "No harm in 2.15 watching the television."

"Maybe not," said Pete Grubb, "but he insists on watching fancy programmes on Ancient Greek architecture and modern music and the like, while me and the missus want to watch soap operas and things."

"Still," said Lucy, "it's not that serious."

"It *is*," insisted Pete Grubb. "On account of that wolf, me and the missus are the only people in the whole world who don't know who shot J.R."

"I'll tell you," offered Lucy. "It was—"

"I don't want you to tell me," interrupted Pete Grubb. "I want to see it myself on my very own telly, just like everyone else."

"Well," said Lucy, "why can't you tell 2.15 that if he comes to watch your TV he's got to watch what everyone else wants to see?"

"I do," said Pete Grubb in an aggrieved tone, "I do, all the time, but he doesn't listen."

"Oh dear," said Lucy. "I don't see how we can help though – I don't suppose he'd take any notice of us, either."

"Well, he better had," snapped Pete Grubb, "because if he doesn't, I'm going to tell on him. I'll go and spill the beans to the local constabulary. I'll tell them all about that wolf that escaped from the zoo."

"You can't!" exclaimed Lucy. "Not after everything 2.15 has done for you, helping you to live happily ever after."

"Never mind about that," said Pete Grubb. "Either he leaves my telly alone or I'll spill the beans. You tell him that, and tell him that I really mean it," and off he stomped, slamming the door.

"I suppose I'll have to take 2.15 to London," sighed Lucy. "If I don't old Grubb will go to the police."

"Looks like it," agreed her mother. "I hope Gran and Grandad won't mind. You'd better go and find him and tell him the news."

So Lucy trudged through the forest in search of 2.15. Eventually she found him, lying under a tree reading out loud to 3.45.

2.15 grinned when he saw Lucy. "Hail to thee, blithe spirit," he called out. "Why the long face?"

"Pete Grubb came to see us," Lucy told him.

"Thought he might," said the wolf.

"Yes," Lucy continued, "and he's very fed up with you because you won't let him watch what *he* wants to watch on television, and he's threatening to go to the police about you and 3.45."

"I'd like to eat that horrid little Pete Grubb for my supper," snapped 3.45.

2.15 laughed. "Then once he was cooked you could say 'Grubb up'," he hooted.

"Oh, you think you're very funny, don't you?" snapped 3.45.

"Well, to be perfectly honest with you, my love, I do," said 2.15. "And you must admit Pete Grubb is an absurd little fellow."

"Absurd he may be," said Lucy, "but he could get us all into a lot of trouble. I think you'd better come to London with me after all, just to keep out of his hair."

"People!" sniffed 3.45. "A waste of time, all of them. A waste of time!" Still, she agreed that it would be safer if 2.15 was away from the forest for a bit, and she reluctantly agreed to let him take the 2.15 to London with Lucy the following Sunday.

"You went off and annoyed old Grubb on purpose," complained 3.45, "so that I would have to give in and let you go off to London."

"My dear, my dear," replied 2.15, smiling fondly, "as if I would do such a thing."

Chapter Two
It Shouldn't Happen to a Dog

The following Sunday Lucy and 2.15 were on the train to London. They sat in the guard's van, chatting.

"Just like the good old days," said 2.15 cheerfully. "The beginning of my saunter down memory lane."

Lucy giggled. "Do you remember all the post you threw around last time, to get the string off the letters to make a collar and lead?"

"I do," said 2.15. "I most certainly do. Let's do it again, just for fun."

"No," said Lucy sternly. "Definitely not."

"Not just one little bag?" wheedled the wolf.

"No," said Lucy. "Now not another word about it."

"Who do you think will meet us at the station?" asked 2.15, rapidly changing the subject. "I *am* looking forward to seeing everyone again. You did tell them I was coming?"

"Of course I did," said Lucy.

"Hmmm," said 2.15. "Then I expect there will be a big crowd to welcome me at the station."

As soon as the train drew into the station 2.15 leapt off and scanned the platform for familiar faces. "There's no one here," he told Lucy plaintively.

"Sssh," said Lucy urgently. "Remember you're supposed to be a dog," and she put his lead on. Then they waited for a while, but no one turned up.

"We'll have to go by tube," Lucy told 2.15.

"All right," whispered the wolf. "But I think it's a very poor show. Here I am returning to the scene of my earlier triumphs, and no one takes any notice."

Eventually they arrived at Gran and Grandad's flat. Grandad answered the door.

"Hello, Lucy," he said, giving her a kiss. "Hello, 2.15. I'd forgotten you were coming."

"Charming," said 2.15 sourly. "Charming, I must say."

Just then Gran came in with the shopping. "Hello, love," she said to Lucy. "Oh my goodness, there's 2.15. You could have told me you were coming. I'd have got in some tins of dog food."

"It wasn't like this before," moaned 2.15. "I wanted a little ramble among my memories, but it seems I had a bad memory. No one wants me here. Well, I don't want to stay where I'm not wanted," and he flounced out, slamming the kitchen door and flinging open the one to the front room. There sat all his old friends: Liz Howes, the social worker; old Mrs Barton, who 2.15 had looked after; all the children he had cared for – Sue, Hugh, Maureen, Doreen and Mike, Sharon, Karen, Darren, Stacey and Wayne; all the lads from Grandad's days in the army; and most of the people who lived in the flats, and in the middle of the table was a cake with *Welcome back, 2.15* written on it in pink icing. 2.15 grinned from ear to ear, and everyone cheered. Then the wolf held up his paw for silence.

"Friends," he said, "dear friends, how wonderful to be among you again. Gran and Grandad, forgive me for doubting you. You are indeed good and loving friends. As one who is living happily ever after, there has been only one thing I have missed when in the forest with my beloved 3.45, and that is the sight of all the dear and wonderful people I knew in London. Before we all get down to eating this wonderful cake, thank you for coming, and I look forward to seeing a lot of you all in the next couple of weeks. Thank you, thank you, thank you."

The party was a great success.

The next day, after cleaning up, Gran asked 2.15 what he wanted to do.

"I want to go up to Oxford Street and buy 3.45 a hat," he told her.

"What on earth would she do with a hat?" asked Gran.

"Wear it, of course," explained 2.15. "What else would she do with it?"

"I only asked," said Gran apologetically.

"Do you want me to come with you?" asked Lucy.

"Well, yes," said 2.15 after a moment's thought. "You might come in handy to try on the hats and to pay for the one I choose."

So the two of them went off together. "Just like the good old days," commented 2.15.

The wolf enjoyed going in and out of the shops, particularly those which had 'No Dogs Allowed' notices. Lucy tried on lots of hats until 2.15 decided on the one he liked best. Lucy was just paying for it when she heard cries all over the shop of, "Stop, thief!" Lucy looked around, but there was no sign of 2.15, and people were running all over the place looking for the thief.

"What's going on?" Lucy asked, hoping desperately that it had nothing to do with 2.15.

"Someone snatched an old lady's handbag," the sales girl told her.

Lucy was relieved. 2.15 wouldn't do a thing like that. She went down the escalator and was just about to walk out of the shop when a man came up to her.

"Excuse me, miss. I'm the store detective. Did you see a dog snatch the old lady's handbag?"

Lucy's heart sank. So 2.15 was involved after all.

"No," she said sincerely. "I didn't see anything."

"Thank you, miss," said the store detective. Lucy smiled and began to push her way through the crowd, hoping to find 2.15. As she came out into the street she looked round.

"Psst," came a voice from a shop doorway. "Quick, over here."

Lucy walked over towards the voice and there, cowering in the shadows, was 2.15.

"Why did you steal the old lady's bag?" Lucy demanded.

"I didn't, silly. Wolves don't steal," hissed 2.15. "A thief took it and I snatched it back from him to give to the old lady, but when she saw me with it she yelled, 'Stop, thief!' and everyone began chasing me. Here's the bag. Go and give it back to her. I'll wait here."

Gingerly Lucy took the bag and went over to the crowd. "Excuse me," she said to a policeman who was taking notes. "Is this the lost bag?"

"That's the one," said the policeman. "Where did you find it?"

"Oh, somewhere in the shop," said Lucy vaguely.

"Any help you can give, miss, we'd be happy to hear about," said the policeman. "I reckon some villain has trained that dog to steal, so we've got to catch it. Now, my description says that the dog is big, with a mangy grey coat and sharp teeth. Have you anything to add to that, young lady?"

"I think it was a small dog with spots," said Lucy, "and hair all over its eyes."

"Wrong dog," said the policeman. "Ten people have described the rogue dog as big and grey. We've got to find the brute before he robs anyone else. I'll send out a general alarm. Every policeman in London will have that dog's description within hours."

Lucy backed away and returned to the doorway where 2.15 was crouching. "Come on," she said. "We've got to get out of here."

They began walking towards the nearest tube station when they heard the sound of police cars.

"We'll never make it," said Lucy, looking round for a way to escape. "Quick, come in here."

"Come in where?" asked 2.15.

"Here, into this dog parlour," said Lucy urgently,

22

dragging him in as a police car screeched past.

"Good morning, madam," said the receptionist in the dog parlour. "Can I help you?"

"Well, yes," said Lucy. "I want my dog to look different."

The receptionist leant over her desk to look at 2.15. "Yes, madam," she said, looking down her nose at the wolf. "I can quite see why you would want him to look different. Ugly animal, isn't he?"

"You're not so hot yourself," muttered 2.15 under his breath.

"May I suggest that we cut his hair very short and leave just a little frill round his neck," suggested the receptionist.

"Would that make him look completely different?" asked Lucy.

"Oh quite," said the receptionist. "His own mother wouldn't recognize him."

2.15 growled.

"Be quiet, 2.15," said Lucy firmly. "Yes, that is what I would like you to do."

"You'd think the dog understood, the way he's carrying on," commented the receptionist. "Come along, doggums, there's a good little doggie."

So 2.15 was clipped and scrubbed and had a red bow tied round his neck, and he was sprayed with perfume. The receptionist looked hard at him as he and Lucy prepared to walk out of the shop.

"He looks a bit better," she remarked, "but he's not what you would call a pretty dog, is he? Still, he looks much better. There's a good doggums then."

"Doggums indeed," growled 2.15. "Let's get out of here."

Out in the street 2.15 pulled Lucy over towards a mirror in a shop window. He looked hard at his own reflection and a tear ran down his nose. "I don't even look like me," he proclaimed miserably. "I look like some silly old pretty doggums."

"I think you look rather good myself," said Lucy, trying hard not to giggle because 2.15 really did look rather odd.

"I shall never forgive you for this," said 2.15 vehemently. "Never, never, never!" and he pulled

himself free of his lead and raced off. Lucy ran after him and eventually she caught up with him in Trafalgar Square. He was rolling around in the rubbish.

"What are you doing?" she asked.

"Grrr," growled 2.15. "Grrr," and he leapt into one of the fountains in the square. Lucy tried to grab him but he was off again, rolling in the rubbish.

"Whatever are you doing?" Lucy asked again.

"I am getting rid of that horrible smell they put on me," snapped 2.15, and he raced off again. Lucy followed him into St James's Park where she found him swimming in the duck pond.

"Come here, 2.15," Lucy shouted at the wolf. After a while he got out of the pond, covered in green slime, and sniffed himself.

"At least I smell like me again," he informed Lucy. "Oh well, nothing else for it. We'd better go home, I suppose."

"I suppose so," agreed Lucy, wondering how Gran and Grandad would react to the new, streamlined 2.15.

As they walked from the tube to the flat they passed lots of local dogs being taken for their evening walks. All the dogs barked at 2.15 and pulled on their leads, turning to stare at him all the way along the road.

"What's going on?" asked Lucy.

"They all think I look very funny," said 2.15

bitterly. "They're all having a good laugh at my expense, and it's all *your* fault."

When they got to the flats they passed the children playing outside in the playground.

"Is that 2.15?" asked Hugh.

"Of course it's me," said 2.15.

Hugh snorted. "You do look funny. Hey, Maureen, come and see 2.15. He's been to the hairdressers'."

"I will not stand here to be a laughing stock," said 2.15 and he stomped off upstairs.

"Whatever happened to you?" asked Grandad, staring at 2.15. Lucy explained. Gran and Grandad roared with laughter.

"Well, you're safe from the police, mate," said Grandad. "No one will take you for the dog in the shop."

"Poor old wolf," said Gran, trying not to laugh. "All for trying to help an old woman to keep her handbag."

"That's right," said 2.15. "3.45 got it right. People *are* a waste of time."

"Maybe you should go back to the forest and 3.45," suggested Lucy.

"Don't be ridiculous," snapped the wolf. "She's the last person, I mean wolf, I want to see me looking like this. She told me not to come up to London. I don't want her falling about with laughter and saying 'I told you so'."

"It may not take long to grow back" said Grandad.

"It had better not," growled 2.15. "And until it does, I shall remain indoors, not wishing to be the subject of public ridicule, fun and derision," and he turned his back on them and lay down with his head on his paws, looking very miserable.

Chapter Three
GASTON LOUP

The next day 2.15 just lay miserably in front of the television, refusing to eat and only going out on his own late at night when it was dark. He refused to speak to Lucy, and when he had to communicate with her it was always through Gran or Grandad.

"You may convey to the person sitting over there that I do not wish to eat anything she has prepared," or "You may tell Miss Lucy that I shall not be needing her services from now on," was all he would say. Lucy got more and more miserable.

One morning 2.15 looked even more fed up than usual.

"What's up, old chap?" asked Grandad.

"It's all her fault," said 2.15. "It's that Lucy, she did this to me."

"What's 'appened now?" enquired Grandad.

"I went to the zoo last night to visit the wolves and to give them messages from 3.45, but as soon as they saw me they began to fall about all over the place too, killing themselves with laughter, lying on their backs and kicking their legs up in the air with merriment. I assure you, sir, that that is how it was. They were rendered helpless with unseemly mirth."

"Did you manage to give them the messages?" asked Grandad.

"I most certainly did not," replied 2.15 huffily. "Now there's no one I can talk to – no people, no dogs, no wolves – and it's all *her* fault."

"Come off it, 2.15," said Grandad. Lucy was only trying to save you. She thought that if she 'adn't taken you into that dogs' beauty parlour you might 'ave been arrested, and then where would you 'ave been?"

"I could have explained," answered 2.15. "The police would have understood."

"I'm not so sure they would," said Grandad. "Lucy did what seemed best for you at the time. I can't believe that all the police would 'ave been after you, they've got so much on their 'ands, but I expect it seemed pretty desperate to Lucy at the time."

"She could at least have asked me what I thought about it," complained the wolf. "After all, it's my coat they shaved off."

"'Ow long do you think it will take to grow?" asked Grandad.

"No idea," sniffed 215. "I've never been to the barber's before. One doesn't when living in the forest, you know."

"Well, I think you and Lucy should make it up. She's dead miserable because you won't talk to her," said Grandad.

"Good," said 2.15. "Let her suffer – it is no less than she deserves."

So 2.15 stayed at home and watched television and sulked. He didn't show much interest in anything until all of a sudden he pepped up.

"I've solved the problem," he cried. "No longer need I languish, lonely and isolated. I can return to the world without being the subject of ridicule and derision."

"What do you mean?" asked Grandad.

"The greyhounds," yelled 2.15. "They will be my salvation."

"But 2.15," said Gran, "you aren't a greyhound, and you can't run like one."

"I know I'm not a greyhound," said 2.15 patiently. "But look at those little jackets the Greyhounds wear. You could get me one of those and then I could sally forth once more and mix with the populace."

So 2.15 was given a small red jacket and, as he put it on, he consented to talk to Lucy.

"I thought you were never going to talk to me again," she told him.

"I never said that I wouldn't talk to you ever again, dear child. What I did say was that I would never forgive you, and that I shall never do, but I'm quite prepared to talk to you now and again. In fact, we could go for a walk now and I can see if my red jacket meets with the approval of the public." So the two went off and, wearing his red jacket, 2.15 attracted far less attention.

"Well, 2.15," said Lucy, "it seems your problem is solved."

"I'm not so sure about that," sniffed the wolf.

"Why not?" asked Lucy.

"My bottom's cold," 2.15 complained. "This little jacket is a bottom freezer. I'm used to having lots of nice warm fur round my rear end. I don't think this jacket is the answer to my problem after all.'

"Oh dear," sighed Lucy, wondering if 2.15 was going to send her to Coventry again.

The next day 2.15 disappeared. Grandad and Lucy asked the neighbours if any of them had seen him but no one had.

"I do 'ope 'ee isn't doing anythin' foolish," said Grandad. "'Ee's been in such a funny mood lately, since 'is little misfortune."

"I know," agreed Lucy. "But at least he's stopped sulking, and I think he's quite tough, a survivor."

There was a knock at the door.

"Maybe it's him," said Lucy, running to answer it, but it turned out to be an onion seller from France. So Lucy bought a bunch of onions and they sat anxiously waiting for 2.15.

"I suppose I'd better go and look for him," said Lucy at last, and she put on her red anorak and off she went. She looked all over the flats and then decided that she'd better go and search in the streets round about. As she turned the corner by the flats she saw a crowd gathering round the French onion seller who was shivering in his short sleeves as he talked to a policeman who had hurried up.

"I'd just 'ad my *dejeuner*, 'ow you say eet? Ah yes, my lunch," said the onion seller with a strong French accent. "I left my *bicyclette* outside ze door and took off my blue beret and my striped jumper and jacket, so zat I could wash myself a leetle and ze next instant zey were gone, *absolument* gone."

"Very odd," commented the policeman. "Did anyone see the culprit?"

"Well," said the café owner, who had joined the crowd, "a very odd sort of chap came into my café, swinging bunches of onions, and I thought there was something a bit funny going on when he asked for snails and chips."

"Snails and chips!" exclaimed the policeman. "It sounds horrible."

"That's what I thought," said the café owner. "I mean, they eat snails in France, but not with chips."

"So what happened next?" asked the policeman.

"Well, when I said that we didn't serve snails and chips, he asked for frogs' legs on toast."

"They eat frogs' legs in France too," commented the policeman.

"But not on toast," replied the café owner.

"Yes," agreed the policeman. "We're obviously dealing with a bit of a joker."

"*Mon dieu*," moaned the onion seller. "When are you going to find zis joker?"

"We're doing our best, sir," the policeman told him. "Now, did anyone else see him?"

"I did," volunteered a woman. "He came and had a cup of tea. Very nice he was, said his name was Gaston Loup. We had a long chat, and he kissed my hand as he left and said I had beautiful eyes. He was very nice, very hairy but very nice."

Lucy's heart sank.

"I'll go and report this to the station," said the policeman. "As soon as I hear anything I'll get in touch."

Lucy went up to the onion seller. "I think I know who took your bike and your onions and your clothes. If you come to my place, I'll see that you get them back."

So, shivering and miserable, the onion seller followed Lucy. When Grandad heard the story he loaned the Frenchman a sweater and made him a big

33

cup of tea while he warmed himself at the fire, and then toasted a mountain of crispy crumpets. The onion seller gratefully drank the tea and ate twelve crumpets.

"Very nice, zis English cake," he remarked.

Lucy stood looking out of the window. In the distance she saw a figure on a bike weaving all the way down the road towards the flats.

"He's coming, Grandad," she said.

"I'll give 'im what for when 'ee walks through that door," said Grandad. "Stealin' the poor man's bike and 'is clothes and 'is onions."

Grandad opened the door and in walked 2.15 wearing the onion seller's striped sweater and jacket and with the beret low over his face and a French cigarette hanging out of his mouth.

"Now you listen 'ere, 2.15," began Grandad. "'Ow dare you steal this poor man's clothes and 'is bike?"

"Dear friend, dear friend," cried 2.15, "pray calm yourself. I did not steal them, I merely borrowed them for a short while. *Cher ami*," he said to the onion seller, "forgive me, but I was so bored that I borrowed your identity for a few brief hours. I'm sorry, but I sold all your onions and here is the money. Now let's shake hands and forget all about it."

The onion seller's eyes grew large in amazement. "Eet ees not a man, eet ees a dog, a *chien qui parle*!"

"*Non, monsieur*," corrected 2.15. "I am not a dog, but a wolf."

"A wolf?" said the Frenchman. "A wolf? *Qu'est qu'on dit en francais?*"

"*Un loup*," said Lucy.

"*Un loup!*" cried the Frenchman, stepping back in alarm.

"*Mais oui, cher ami*," said 2.15. "But not any old wolf. I am the wolf from *Red Riding Hood*."

"*Le chaperon rouge?!*" exclaimed the Frenchman. "But then you are an old friend. Always I 'ave loved that story and often I read eet to *mes enfants*, to my children. Ah, *quelle chose*. Just wait till I tell my wife and children. And now I see why you called yourself Gaston Loup."

"That's right," said 2.15. "Gaston Wolf in English."

"But zis is all wonderful," said the onion seller. "I would like to cook you all a French meal to celebrate this unexpected meeting."

2.15 was thrilled at the thought of eating a French meal. "Ah," he said, "at last I can sample the delights of snails and frogs' legs."

"I'm not eatin' anything like that," said Grandad firmly.

"Ugh," agreed Lucy. "They sound horrible."

"*Cher ami*," said the onion seller to the wolf, "I do not think it will be easy to get such things at your local *supermarché*. I think we will have to make something a little more, 'ow you say eet, conventional."

"Point taken," said 2.15. "But may I accompany you to purchase this meal and at least have some say in the choice of ingredients?"

"*Mais oui*, certainly," said the onion seller.

"You'll have to go to the market then," said Gran. "No dogs allowed in the shops."

"No dogs allowed," moaned 2.15. "That's all I hear. I shall have to start an organization to protect dogs' rights. Still, if the shops will not let me in, they do not deserve my custom. To the market let us go."

So 2.15 put on his jacket and soon he and Lucy and the onion seller were pushing their way through the crowded market. They had great fun buying lots of delicious food, and all the stall holders greeted the onion seller.

"Glad to 'ear you got yer bike and yer clothes back, mate," called one.

"All worked out all right then?" asked another.

"'Ang about," said a third one, "and we'll go and 'ave a drink together."

The Frenchman was delighted. "Never 'ave so many people spoken with me on my trips to England. Eet ees wonderful, *c'est merveilleux*."

"There is nothing like a wolf to help you live happily," commented 2.15 proudly. "Now, let us return to our abode and proceed with the cooking of all this splendid fare."

When they returned, the Frenchman cooked them all a wonderful meal and they drank wine and toasted everyone, and everyone was invited to come and stay in France for as long as they liked.

"I 'ave been coming to England now for many years," said the onion seller, "but zis ees ze first time I get to know any people among ze English. Usually I just sell my onions and stay in an 'otel, but zis time I meet people and my old friend *le loup*, oh *c'est merveilleux. Merci mille fois*, 2.15. You 'ave made me very 'appy. Now always I will look forward to my trips to Angleterre. Another toast to my friends, *vive l'Angleterre, vive le loup*!"

Chapter Four
GUISEPPE LUPO

After the French onion seller had gone, 2.15
finished the bottle of wine, drank four cups of
coffee and informed Gran, Grandad and Lucy
that for the first time since he'd had his hair cut
he felt in a good mood.

"Well, I don't," announced Gran. "When I
came home and heard that the police had been
around the flats asking questions I nearly died."

"Dear lady, dear lady," said 2.15, "I simply
can't imagine why you are agitated – after all,
what harm was done? I had a bit of fun, I made
the day of many a lady by kissing her hand and
telling her she was beautiful, I sold all the onions
and we got an invitation to visit France. So
where, I ask you, is the harm in that?"

"It's just that with you around, 2.15, I never
know what is going to happen next. I mean,
ordinarily I go to work, do the shopping, come
home and Grandad has my supper ready, then we
sit down and watch a bit of television and then we
go to bed. But with you around, life gets so
unpredictable. It's one thing after another."

2.15 put his nose in her lap. "And you love it.
Go on, admit it, you love it when I'm around and
lots of people come in and everyone has lots of
fun. You enjoyed running circles round old Pete

Grubb last time, didn't you? Come on now, be honest," he wheedled.

"Well," said Gran, softening a bit, "I admit it is livelier, and at least we don't have Pete Grubb to worry about any more, but I'm getting a bit old for all the excitement, 2.15."

"Dear lady, it is not for much longer. Shortly you will leave this place for a much-earned retirement in the quiet of the forest. I myself am here to help with your departure. However, until you go, I feel a little excitement here and a little action there will add some spice to your life."

"Spice indeed," snorted Grandad. "You'll land us all in prison, I can see it coming. I don't know why we let you come back."

"Fear not, dear friend," cried the wolf, "for you know that I am committed to making sure that everyone lives happily ever after. Cast your mind back – for you and Gran I got a cottage in the forest; Lucy was freed from a life in front of the television; 3.45 was rescued from the zoo; and even Pete Grubb is happy with his widow. No, dear friend, I do not present a threat to your well-being."

For all 2.15's grand speeches, Gran, Grandad and Lucy did not feel very reassured.

"The problem is," pronounced Grandad, "that 2.15 is bored, but 'ee's scared of being laughed at if 'ee goes outside, so my guess is that we can expect another little disguise soon."

It didn't take long for Grandad's prediction to come true. As it was getting very near to Christmas, Lucy and Grandad went to do some Christmas shopping the next morning. They went up to Oxford Street and enjoyed the lights and the crowds and the bustle.

"The last time I was here," Lucy told her grandfather, "was the time that I bought the hat for 3.45 and 2.15 had his… er… haircut."

"Don't think about that, love," said Grandad. "You're 'ere to enjoy yourself. Come on, let's go in 'ere and find the toy department, and see what presents Santa is givin' out."

So they took the lift up to the fourth floor and there, under a huge Christmas tree, was Father Christmas giving out gifts and singing and chatting to the large crowd of children.

"There's something familiar about that Father Christmas," said Lucy.

"Don't talk so daft," said her grandfather. "It's an actor or someone dressed up in a red 'ood, that's all."

"I don't think so," said Lucy. "Look at his hands."

Grandad looked and, sure enough, sticking out from the red sleeves with their fur cuffs were two grey paws.

"Oh no," groaned Grandad, "I can't stand it."

"Little girl," the Father Christmas called out to Lucy. "Come here, my cherub, and let me give you a present."

Lucy went over to 2.15 and he put her on his knee.

"I know it's you, 2.15," she whispered in his ear.

"I'm having a wonderful time," he told her. "I like children. Now as you're my favourite child, you pick a present out of my sack." And while Lucy chose a gift 2.15 sang at the top of his voice:

"I'm dreaming of a white Christmas
Just like the ones I used to know."

Lucy had just selected a large gift wrapped in green paper when she looked up and saw the familiar figure of the store detective. Next to him was a man wearing a coat over his underwear.

"I think they've rumbled you, 2.15," she said quietly. "There's the store detective over there."

"Oh dear," said the wolf. "And the man next to him is the real Santa Claus. I borrowed his clothes."

"We'd better run for it," said Lucy.

So, holding hands, they raced through the toy department and down the escalators. 2.15 stopped off for a minute in the dress department to rush into a cubicle and take off the Father Christmas outfit. A woman who was in the cubicle trying on some clothes fainted with shock. Looking like any ordinary girl with her dog, Lucy and 2.15 got home on public transport. Grandad arrived a bit later.

"You're takin' such risks, 2.15," said Grandad. "I think you've gone barmy."

"Not at all, dear friend," said the wolf. "I am merely enjoying myself in a wolfish sort of way."

That afternoon Hugh, Sue, Maureen, Doreen and Mike dropped by to tell Lucy that there was an ice-cream van outside and that the ice-cream man was giving away ice-cream for free.

"For free!" said Lucy, amazed. "What's he doing that for?"

"He's an Italian," explained Hugh.

"Yes," said Maureen. "His name's Giuseppe Lupo."

"And," went on Doreen, "he loves children. *'Bambini',* he calls us."

"That's Italian for children," interrupted Sue.

"So he's giving all the *bambini* free ice-cream," concluded Mike.

"It sound very odd to me," said Lucy suspiciously.

"Never mind that," insisted the children. "Come and get your free ice-cream before it's all gone."

So Lucy raced downstairs with the others and there was the ice-cream van with *Come back to Sorrento* blasting out and 2.15 dressed up in the ice-cream man's cap and apron handing out ice-creams.

"Ah," he was saying to a little blonde girl. "Ah, *la piccola biondina*, you wanta chocolate, strawberry, lemon and vanilla? I giva you chocolate, strawberry, lemon and vanilla – *molto bene*."

Lucy's heart sank as 2.15 gave out ice-cream

after ice-cream, singing *Arrivederci, Roma* at the top of his voice and blowing kisses to everyone.

In the distance Lucy could hear a police siren. "2.15," she whispered, "the police are coming. Quick, drive the van round the corner and then nip upstairs as fast as you can."

"No more ice-cream today, *bambini*," yelled 2.15. "*Scusi*, but Giuseppe Lupo must move off pretty quick. *Arrivederci*, I lova you all. *Scusi, scusi*." And as the children scattered the van clattered off. As soon as it was parked, 2.15 leapt out and as Lucy ran up he pulled off his apron and his hat and rushed upstairs yelling, "There's just enough coffee ice-cream left for one," as the police car screeched round the corner. A policeman got out with another man.

"Is that your ice-cream van, Mr de Marco?" asked the policeman.

"Yes, that's it," said Mr De Marco looking inside. "Nothing's been damaged, but all the ice-cream's gone."

"Very odd," said the policeman. "I've never heard of an ice-cream thief before." Just then he caught sight of Lucy trying to slip quietly away. "Just a minute, miss. What do you know about all this?"

"Nothing," said Lucy honestly, "except that someone has been giving away ice-creams for free."

"Giving them away?" said Mr de Marco. "Giving away five hundred pounds' worth of ice-cream? Officer, we are dealing with a nut!"

"So it would seem, sir," agreed the policeman. "And you, young lady, you always seem to be around when this sort of thing happens. What do you know about this theft, and the onion seller's bicycle?"

"You don't think it's me that takes things, do you?" asked Lucy.

"No, of course not," answered the policeman. "But I'd bet my bottom dollar that you know the man's name as does it."

Lucy breathed a sigh of relief. She looked into

the policeman's eyes and said, "Honestly, I do not know the name of any man who steals bicycles or ice-cream vans."

"She's telling the truth," said Mr de Marco. "She doesn't know what the fellow is called."

"Well, I still think she's mixed up in this somehow," said the policeman. "She's always around when something odd happens. I'll be round to see your grandad later tonight, young lady."

Lucy rushed home and told 2.15 what had happened. 2.15 was upset when Lucy told him about Mr de Marco and the five hundred pounds.

"Oh dear," he cried. "Poor man, and I don't have any money left to pay him back, and we can't do The Amazing Lucy Jones and her Performing Dog Show because I'm not having people laugh at me. Oh dear, the poor man. He and Mrs de Marco and all the little de Marcos will be living on bread and water for a month."

"Well, you'll have to find a way of getting the money to repay him, won't you?" pronounced Lucy. "And if you don't stop all this nonsense, 2.15, you'll get caught. That policeman was very suspicious. He's coming round later."

"Don't give it another thought," said 2.15 blithely. "He won't suspect me for a minute."

Later that evening the policeman came round. Gran, Grandad and Lucy were all very anxious, but 2.15 lay on the floor happily doing a puzzle and singing *Arrivederci, Roma*. As the policeman came into the room, Lucy slipped on to the floor and took over the puzzle, and whispered fiercely to 2.15, "Be quiet!" 2.15 grinned and gave her a big wet lick, and lay down like a dog.

The policeman apologized for bothering Gran and Grandad, who agreed that the recent crimes were very odd indeed and that it was difficult to understand what was behind them. Gran offered the policeman a cup of tea and went off to the kitchen, and the policeman sat down. 2.15 trotted over and put his paw on the policeman's knee.

"Hello, boy," said the policeman. "Good dog." 2.15 licked the policeman's hand.

"Isn't this the dog you used to bring into the pub?" asked the policeman.

"That's the one," said Grandad. "He's my granddaughter Lucy's dog."

"He looks very odd," commented the policeman. "What happened to him?"

"'Ee 'ad fleas," said Grandad quickly, "very bad fleas, and the vet said 'ee 'ad to be shaved, so shaved 'ee was."

2.15 glared at Grandad accusingly.

"Does he still like crisps?" asked the policeman.

"I imagine so," said Grandad.

So the policeman got out a packet of crisps and fed them all to 2.15 while he told them all about the extraordinary events that had occurred in the area and how puzzled he was. 2.15 felt a bit guilty about all the trouble and confusion he was causing and put his head into the policeman's lap.

"Amazing, isn't it?" said the policeman. "You'd almost think he was sympathizing with me. Good dog."

Chapter Five
Sir Samuel Wolf

After the incident with Giuseppe Lupo and the free ice-cream, Gran, Grandad and Lucy were very cross with 2.15. This didn't bother him very much, but he continued to worry in case the de Marco family were living on bread and water. However, soon after the policeman's visit something happened which put 2.15 and his problems out of everybody's minds. It had been announced that the whole area was to be redeveloped with office blocks to make way for the overflow from the City of London. No one talked about anything else. Liz Howes, the social worker, came over to talk about it with Gran and Grandad.

"We've got to organize," she said to Gran and Grandad. "There's going to be a meeting at the church hall. Everyone is coming. You will be there, won't you?"

"I don't know about that," said Grandad. "I'm gettin' on, you know, and I'm movin' out at the end of the month."

"Honestly, Bert," said Gran, "I'm surprised at you. You've lived round here all your life. You just give a thought to all the people who aren't lucky enough to have 2.15 to help them raise money for a cottage in the country."

"Here, here," said 2.15 resoundingly. "I'll second that any time."

"That's all well and good," groaned Grandad, "but I'm no good at protestin' and that. Even that wolf can get me to do what 'ee wants. All I want is a quiet life."

"Don't you worry, Liz," interrupted 2.15. "He'll be at the meeting, I warrant. You have my word as a wolf and a gentleman."

"That's right," agreed Gran. "Don't you worry about it, Liz."

"If I may interject a moment," said 2.15, "could some kind soul explain to me why this development is such a bad thing. After all, no offence intended, but it's not very wonderful round here at the moment."

"True," said Liz Howes, "but this plan won't help the people of the area at all. It will just make a lot of money for Sir Samuel Wolf. What this area needs are parks, a play area for the children, a swimming pool and more homes."

"That's right," agreed Gran. "And more shops, so that you don't have to carry heavy shopping for miles."

"Yes," said Grandad, "and places for the old people to go, rather than sit around all alone in cold homes."

"I see," said 2.15. "And if these office blocks get built by this wolf, you won't get any of these things?"

"That's the point," said Liz. "All those extra people working here and earning money will put the prices of things up and make places more crowded – buses and so on – but apart from helping the local shops, the area won't benefit at all."

"I know," said 2.15. "I know what to do. It's very simple. I'll challenge this wolf to single combat and I'll go for his throat and I'll chew his ears off and bite his tail and then he'll see sense and do what you want."

Liz Howes laughed, "He's not that kind of wolf, 2.15," she said.

"Then what kind of wolf is he?" demanded 2.15.

"He's a person," said Gran.

2.15 groaned. "I should have known," he said.

"You're beginning to sound like 3.45," commented Lucy.

"Never mind sounding like her," said 2.15, "I'm beginning to feel like her!" The wolf sat down to think. After a few minutes he spoke again.

"But surely, if you explained this to Sir Samuel Wolf, he would understand. It must be that he is unaware of these issues. You must bring them to his notice. I myself could approach him, as a fellow wolf, (when my coat has grown a little) and appraise him of the facts."

"No point," said Liz Howes gloomily. "We have

been told that the locals will not be consulted. They say the scheme will bring money and employment to the area."

"It's an outrage," shouted 2.15. "An outrage is what I call it. Not to ask the local people what they want when they have to live there. I myself shall attend the protest meeting."

"But 2.15," said Gran, "you know how unhappy you feel about going out since your visit to the... er... barber."

"Madam," announced the wolf, "there are times when there are more important matters to be taken into account than vanity."

So the following evening Gran, Grandad, Liz Howes and Lucy sat in a row in the packed church hall. There was some fuss about allowing 2.15 in until the man at the door realized that it *was* 2.15 and not some ordinary dog.

"Sorry, mate," he said to the wolf, "but I wouldn't have recognized you in a month of Sundays. Didn't realize you'd become a flippin' skin-head."

2.15 decided to ignore the insult and sat quietly at Gran's feet to listen to the speaker.

At the end of the meeting the chairman said, "Any questions or comments from the floor before we elect our Local Residents' Action Group?"

"Yes," shouted 2.15. "When are you lot going to stop talking and start acting?"

"That you, Bert?" called the Chairman. "Come

on, stand up so that everyone can hear you."

Reluctantly Grandad stood up.

"That's right, Bert," yelled someone. "You tell 'em. You've lived round here long enough."

Grandad coughed and shuffled his feet. "Friends," he said, "I do 'ope you're not going to do anything rash and er…"

At this point 2.15 called out. "Because, er, to be effective and to get through to Sir Samuel Wolf we must be determined, hard-working and above all, well-organized."

"Good old Bert," yelled everyone. "That's telling 'em."

Grandad smiled and looked confused.

"Everyone here must make a contribution," continued 2.15. "No man, woman or child must shirk his part in the coming struggle."

"Hurray!" yelled the crowd. "Bert for secretary of the Save our Community Campaign."

Grandad stared at Gran in despair and then sat down. "You leave this to me, Bert," she said reassuringly.

Gran stood up. "Friends," she said, "my husband is overwhelmed by your show of support. Of course, as one of the few people in this hall born and raised in this part, he is delighted to accept the honour of being your secretary."

"Good old Bert and Mavis," yelled the crowd.

"And," continued Gran, "I shall give up my job and work to save the community until we leave for the country, by which time I think I can safely promise you that Sir Samuel Wolf will have agreed to consultation and co-operation rather than conflict and confrontation."

"Cor blimey, Mavis," whispered Grandad. "Was that you or 2.15?"

"Me, Bert," said Gran, smiling at all the applause. "I surprised myself, but I feel so strongly on this issue I just found the right words."

As they filed out of the hall, lots of people came and shook Gran and Grandad's hands and said, "I'm behind you all the way, Bert," or "Any help you need, Mavis, just call on me every time," and "I'll call round tomorrow, love, and see if you need a hand."

The next morning they all sat round, trying to decide what to do.

"We'll need to get everyone to join the campaign," said Gran. "Everyone who can must pay a subscription to help pay for expenses and publicity."

"Yes," agreed Liz Howes, "and we must get a flyer printed and put one through every letter box."

"I could organize the children to do that," volunteered Lucy. "I'll tell Sue, Hugh, Doreen, Maureen and Mike and they can tell the others."

"Who could design the flyer and the poster?" asked Liz Howes.

"Grandad," said Gran.

"Me?" protested Grandad. "Come off it, Mavis. I 'aven't done anything like that for years."

"Well, it's time you did," said Gran. "You used to be really good at drawing and that, and you were in the printing trade. Now, you get on and do the design, and then go round to your old works and see if they'll do the printing for free, seeing as it's for the community."

"Well," muttered Grandad, "I suppose I'll 'ave a go, but I 'aven't done anything like that since I was a boy." He went into the kitchen and soon came back with a rough draft for the flyer.

"Just a first outline, you understand," he explained apologetically as he showed it to Gran and the helpers.

"Smashing, Bert," said Gran. "I knew you could do it. Now take it round to the printers and take 2.15 with you, he could do with a walk."

So Grandad and 2.15 set off together and Grandad persuaded his old workmates to do the work for free.

"It's for the community, you see," he explained. "Now, you all work here and some of you live 'ere an' all, so you owe it to yourselves to do the job for nothing."

"Well said," whispered 2.15.

Soon everyone was convinced and they agreed to work for nothing. 2.15 and Grandad, feeling pleased with themselves, set off to tell the good news to the Committee.

"You know," said Grandad, "it's a funny thing, but I feel ten years younger, and Mavis, bless 'er, is just like a young thing since we took on this campaign."

"'Course you do," said 2.15, "'cos you're helping people to live happily ever after."

The campaign went on and everybody worked very hard. 2.15 rang Sir Samuel Wolf's secretary and tried to get an appointment for Sir Samuel Wolf to see Gran and Grandad and the Committee, but every time 2.15 was informed

that Sir Samuel was not interested in the Committee's views and would the Committee please stop pestering him.

Meanwhile, Sir Samuel's company began to buy up all the old warehouses and buildings near the River Thames that were no longer in use. Despite all their hard work, the Committee and their supporters began to feel that the struggle was hopeless.

"He's bought up all the land," Gran told 2.15. "He'll be able to do whatever he likes."

"Dear friends," said 2.15, seeing their disconsolate faces, "do not give way to despair, do not become disheartened. We shall find a way to defeat this Sir Samuel Wolf. It takes a wolf to defeat a wolf. Leave it to me. *Au revoir*, dear friends, *au revoir*, but not goodbye," and, blowing kisses to the Committee, he ran off.

Late that night 2.15 had not returned. Gran, Grandad and Lucy were worried.

"'Ee's up to something," said Grandad. "I can feel it in me bones."

"Me too," said Gran. "I hope he's gone to tell that Sir Samuel Wolf what he thinks of him."

At that moment the phone rang.

"Maybe it's him," said Gran, falling over Grandad and Lucy who were both clambering to answer it.

"Hello," said Gran. "Oh, hello, Liz, we thought it might be 2.15. No, he's not back here yet. Why? What? Kidnapped? Serves him right. All right. Well, as soon as we hear anything we'll let you know.

"That was Liz," explained Gran. "She says it was on the news that Sir Samuel Wolf has been kidnapped."

"Oh dear," moaned Grandad, "I knew that wolf was up to no good."

"We don't *know* it's 2.15," said Lucy.

"That's right," said Grandad. "Let's not jump to conclusions. Maybe someone kidnapped Sir Samuel for money."

"Doesn't sound like it," announced Gran

cheerfully. "I've just been listening to the radio and it says the chauffeur had his clothes stolen, and that the kidnapper drove Sir Samuel away in his own Rolls Royce disguised as a chauffeur."

"2.15," said Lucy grinning. "It must be 2.15 dressed up as the chauffeur."

"Oh dear, oh lor'," said Grandad. "'Ee's gone too far this time with his dressin' up and disguises."

Gran smiled as she picked up her knitting. "I shouldn't worry too much, Bert. I expect 2.15 knows what he's doing, and I wouldn't be in Sir Samuel Wolf's shoes tonight, not for all the tea in China!"

Chapter Six
Cub's Honour

At the very moment when Gran made her statement about not wanting to be in Sir Samuel's shoes, Sir Samuel was in fact sitting and looking at 2.15 amid the rubbish in one of his own warehouses.

"You can take off that silly disguise," said Sir Samuel sourly. "You don't scare me, dressed up as some kind of a cross between a wolf and a dog."

"Not a cross with anything," said 2.15. "Just a wolf."

"Well, take that animal mask off anyway," snapped the millionaire. "You look like something out of a pantomime."

"My dear chap," replied 2.15, "I appreciate that it may be hard for you to grasp this, but I am not in disguise. This is I, 2.15. I understand your confusion for recently I was inadvertently taken to the barber (to avoid being apprehended by the police for a theft I did not commit), but I assure you I am wearing no disguise."

"Do you expect me to believe that you're some kind of wolf sitting talking to me?" asked Sir Samuel.

"I'm not some kind of wolf," replied 2.15 with dignity. "I am *the* wolf. I am the wolf from *Red Riding Hood*."

"In that case," said Sir Samuel, "you should be engaged in eating grandmothers and not in kidnapping millionaires."

"I know, I know," agreed 2.15, "but one has to keep up with the times. Anyway, Gran won't have it and she's very nice – once you get to know them you just can't eat them."

"Are you going to eat me?" asked Sir Samuel.

"Well, to tell you the truth," said 2.15, "I haven't decided. On the one hand it's very tempting, but on the other hand you are very old and scrawny."

"If you don't want to eat me," said the millionaire, "then you must want money."

"Oh no," said 2.15, "I don't want your money. Though I do have a small debt of five hundred pounds and, if you were to help pay it, purely as a loan of course, I would be grateful." The millionaire put his hand into his coat pocket and took out his cheque book. "Who do I make it payable to?" he asked.

"Mr de Marco," said 2.15. "Five hundred pounds to Mr de Marco."

"Ah," cried the millionaire, "so that's your name – de Marco!"

"Oh no," said 2.15 quickly. "I'm not Mr de Marco. Mr de Marco is the ice-cream man whose van I borrowed, and I gave away five hundred pounds' worth of ice-cream to the children. So you see, if I don't give Mr de Marco the money I owe him, he and Mrs de Marco and their children will have to live off bread and water for a month. Right?"

"You're out of your mind!" proclaimed Sir Samuel. "That's what it is – you're deranged. Just my luck to be kidnapped by a wolf, and as if that weren't bad enough, he turns out to be mad as well."

"Not at all," said 2.15. "Not at all, I merely brought you here to persuade you to consult the residents of this area on this nature of the redevelopment scheme you're planning."

"What's all that got to do with you?" sneered the millionaire.

"It's got a lot to do with me. Many of my friends will be affected by this scheme, and what's more, your name is Wolf and that makes me very angry. I have our reputation to think of. You're a disgrace to our name, Sir Samuel, and I refuse to allow this slur on our good reputation to continue. So you can just stay here until you agree to build more houses in your scheme, and a park and a playground and good shops, and facilities for the old and disabled.

"No way!" cried Sir Samuel. "Never!"

"As soon as you agree to that you can go, free as a bird. I don't want to keep you here," continued 2.15. "To be honest, I don't like you very much."

"Let me assure you," snapped Sir Samuel, "that the feeling is mutual. But don't think that I'll give in to you. I'm not scared of you!"

"Look at it like this," said 2.15. "Let's talk, wolf to wolf. You want to make a profit out of these buildings, and I want you to think about the local people who have lived here all their lives. This is their home, their community."

"Oh, I see," sneered Sir Samuel. "You're one of those romantics who goes on about the 'good old days'. You just don't like any sort of change. Well, let me tell you something. I grew up round here, and I remember the 'good old days' and they weren't so good. Kids ill from lack of the right food, huge families crammed into small houses, kids sent out to work long hours when they were fourteen, outdoor lavatories – oh, it wasn't so wonderful, I can tell you. You think I'm just putting up those office blocks for profit, but I'm not. Nothing wrong with profit, but I want to wipe out those slums. I want fine, soaring buildings where there was once just misery and waste."

"Hah," said 2.15. "More complicated than I had first envisaged. But, sir, look at it like this. Why not do away with slums and create an environment that people want to live in?"

"How am I supposed to find out what people want?" snapped Sir Samuel. "I haven't lived here for forty years. When I was a lad my young brother died of tuberculosis because of our living conditions. I swore to get rich and get out of here. This is the first time I've been back in forty years."

"How can you know anything about a place if you haven't been back these forty years?" cried 2.15. "Come, sir, agree to consult the Residents' Action Committee and we can all go round to Gran's. She'll cook you a lovely supper and then you can go home."

"Never!" cried the millionaire. "I will not give in to pressure and blackmail. I'm not worried. The police will find me soon enough."

"Frankly, sir, I doubt it," said 2.15. "After all, they won't be looking for me, will they? And what's more, I'm on very good terms with the police – they give me crisps."

"Crisps?" said the millionaire weakly.

"That's right," explained 2.15. "They think I'm a dog and they give me crisps."

"Oh," said Sir Samuel. "So who does know that you're a wolf?"

"Lots of people," said 2.15. "At first it was only Lucy, and then Gran and Grandad and some of the people in the flats, and then the lads from Grandad's commando group and all the people who I helped fill in forms, and most of the children on the estate, and Liz Howes the social worker. But they're all my mates."

"It's all very puzzling," moaned the millionaire.

"Not really," replied 2.15. "You see, they all like me because I help them to live happily ever after. Grandad and the lads even helped me rescue 3.45."

"Who's 3.45?" asked the millionaire, scratching his head and looking confused.

"She's my wife," said 2.15. "She used to live in the zoo but I rescued her, and now we live in the forest."

"I didn't know wolves had wives," said Sir Samuel.

"Oh yes," said 2.15. "Don't you have a wife?"

"Five," said Sir Samuel.

"Five?" said 2.15 in amazement. "What, all at once?"

"No," replied the millionaire, "not all at once, one at a time. All they wanted was my money. Not one of them loved me for myself."

"Are you married now?" asked 2.15.

"Yes," said Sir Samuel, "but I never see her. I just work and work and earn money and she spends it. I expect she'll be pleased when she hears I've been kidnapped."

"Don't say that, sir," cried 2.15. "I'm sure the fair maid's heart will be broken. Shall I get a message to her saying that you are alive and well?"

"Don't bother," said Sir Samuel gloomily. "Much she cares."

"Oh dear," sighed 2.15. "I can see that I'm going to have my work cut out seeing to it that *you* live happily ever after."

"Are you going to keep me here?" asked the millionaire.

"Certainly," replied 2.15. "Why not?"

"It's cold," complained Sir Samuel, "and damp and empty, and there's no water and it's dirty and where would I sleep?"

"On the floor" said 2.15, "like me."

"Forget it," snapped the millionaire. "I haven't slept on the floor since I was in the army, and I don't intend starting now."

"Well," said 2.15 reasonably, "it's all in your own hands. You can stay here in comfort, or you can stay here cold, miserable and hungry. It's up to you."

"Aha," said the millionaire. "Food. I've got you there. I might get hungry, but you'd get hungry too."

"That is true," said 2.15. "That is perfectly true, but I've got my dinner right here. That is, unless my dinner decides to be reasonable and make a deal with me."

"Get away," sneered the millionaire. "You wouldn't eat me."

"I most certainly would," said 2.15, licking his lips. "It would all depend on how hungry I was. In fact, I'm a bit peckish at this moment. So, what do you say – a dinner or a deal?"

Sir Samuel stared at the wolf in amazement, unable to make a decision.

"OK," growled the wolf, "c'mon now, c'mon, c'mon, c'mon, stop messing around. It's a simple decision you have to make – a dinner or a deal."

The millionaire groaned. "I don't want to make a deal but I don't want to be your dinner either. You've just made me an offer I can't refuse. All right, what's the deal?"

"All you have to do," explained 2.15, "is give me some money to fix this place up nicely, and promise not to try to escape."

"Of course I'll try to escape!" shouted Sir Samuel. "It's my duty to try and escape."

"All right," said 2.15. "So dinner it is and no deal," and he began walking towards Sir Samuel with his tongue hanging out.

"No," yelled Sir Samuel, "I promise!"

"Were you in the Boy Scouts?" asked 2.15.

"None of your business!" snapped the millionaire.

"Were you?" persisted 2.15.

"Well, as a matter of fact I was, but what's that got to do with anything?"

"If you were a Boy Scout then you were a Wolf Cub first?"

"Yes," said the millionaire, trying to be patient.

"Well, then," said 2.15 triumphantly, "I can put you on your Cub's honour not to try to escape."

"If I do agree on Cub's honour not to try to escape, what then?"

"Ah, then," cried 2.15, "what a garden of delights will be yours – a bed, carpets, television, water

heater, books, records, newspapers, as much food as
you want, a view over the river and me for company.
What more could the heart and mind desire?"

"I could do without the company," complained Sir
Samuel, "but the rest sounds all right."

"Good," said 2.15, "so a deal it is and not a dinner.
I knew that underneath you were a reasonable sort of
chap. Bound to be with a name like Wolf. I can see
that we won't be here for long. You'll see the logic of
consulting with the good townsfolk in no time. Now,
give me some money. Good, five hundred pounds
will do for starters. I'll keep the receipts, everything
honest and above board."

The millionaire counted out the money and gave it to 2.15. "I've got to hand it to you," said Sir Samuel, "you drive a hard bargain. No one else has got that much money out of me for forty years."

"And this is only the beginning," cried the wolf. "Soon you will be a happy man not bothered about such things. Now, raise your hand and say, "I, Samuel Wolf, swear on my honour as a former Wolf Cub that I will not attempt to escape or in any way disturb the peace of mind of the great wolf, 2.15."

Sir Samuel wasn't too keen on the 'great wolf' bit, but eventually he took the oath and 2.15 pranced out of the warehouse to get the things he needed to turn the warehouse into a home for himself and the other Wolf.

Chapter Seven
Mr Aladdin

2.15 raced round to Gran and Grandad's as fast as he could.

"'Ere comes trouble," said Grandad sourly.

"2.15," cried Lucy, "are you all right?"

"Is that you, 2.15?" called Gran from the front room where she was putting pamphlets into piles.

"Hello there," called the wolf. "Yes, it's me, and I'm fine."

"Glad someone is," sniffed Grandad. "We've 'ad the police round the flats again, askin' if we knew anythin' about the disappearance of this Sir Samuel Wolf."

"Well, you didn't," said 2.15, "so nothing to worry about."

"I have the feeling that you know something about it, though, 2.15," said Gran.

"My good woman," replied the wolf, smiling, "I not only know something about it, I know everything about it!"

"I knew it was you," said Gran. "You clever old wolf. Well done!"

"Well done?" snapped Grandad. "Well done? 'Ee's gone over the top. 'Ee's gone too far this time."

"Don't be silly, Bert," said Gran. "It's all in a good cause. Where is he, 2.15?"

"In a warehouse down by the river. He's agreed not

to try to escape on his Cub's honour and I've come to get some things to make him more comfortable."

"Like what?" asked Gran.

"Here's a list," said the wolf, "and five hundred pounds to pay for it all. You can get some second-hand stuff. I do not anticipate a long stay for the gentleman, for already I detect a change in his attitude to the community."

"Oh, 2.15, you're wonderful," said Gran, and she kissed him on the nose.

"Madam," said the wolf, "I cannot find it in myself to disagree with you."

"Wonderful?" sulked Grandad. "Barmy, more like."

"I think 2.15 is very good to put himself in danger like this to help the community," said Lucy. "There's nothing in it for him, and I think we should give him as much help as he needs."

"You're both off your rockers as well," pronounced Grandad.

"2.15," continued Lucy, "if there's anything I can do to help, just say. Then I can stop feeling bad about the haircut."

"Right," said 2.15. "You can come with me and help organize the food and, since Grandad does not approve of my project, madam – would you arrange to have these items delivered?" and he handed Gran the list.

"You'll be seen," objected Grandad, "and then they'll be on to you, and then you'll be locked up like you deserve."

"Oh, be quiet, Bert," said Gran. "You're a real wet blanket these days. Don't worry, 2.15. I'll be round at about midnight. Don't take any notice of old misery here."

Lucy and 2.15 set off back to the warehouse.

"What are you going to do about food?" asked Lucy.

"Not sure yet," said 2.15. "But I'm very peckish." So they bought ten packets of crisps and four bars of chocolate and took them back to the warehouse. Sir Samuel was still there and they gave him three packets of crisps and two bars of chocolate.

"I'd love a cup of tea," he said wistfully.

"We've got a primus," said Lucy. "I'll bring it round, and some milk and tea and sugar."

"Fine," said 2.15, "but we will need another source of nourishing food. We can't cook proper meals on a primus."

"You'll have to eat takeaways," said Lucy.

"Umm," said 2.15. "But it might invite suspicion if you go and buy takeaways twice a day."

"You'd better think of something quickly," groaned Sir Samuel, "because I'm starving!" 2.15 gave him the extra bag of crisps and thought hard.

"I've got it," he cried. "In yonder street there is a restaurant run by Aladdin, the one with the magic lamp. I'll go and get food from him. He, like myself, is a character out of a fairy tale. He will support me in this difficult time," and off he ran.

"What's he on about?" Sir Samuel asked Lucy.

"I don't know," answered Lucy. "He gets hold of the wrong end of the stick sometimes. I'd better go and see what he's up to. Remember you're on your Cub's honour."

Lucy followed 2.15 down the road. When she got to the Aladdin Indian Restaurant 2.15 was sitting at a table with the owner eating poppadums.

"Lucy," cried 2.15, "meet my new friend Mr Al-u-Din."

"You mean he's not Aladdin?"

"No," said 2.15, "I erred, he is not Aladdin but Mr Al-u-Din. But no matter, he is a friend. It would have been a treat to meet another character out of a fairy tale, but instead I have a new and trusted friend."

"Yes indeed," said Mr Al-u-Din. "This Sir Samuel wishes to pull down my restaurant. I am not happy about this at all, so I am very pleased to provide delicious Indian food for the duration of the gentleman's confinement."

"Mr Al-u-Din knows the story of *Red Riding Hood*," said 2.15 excitedly.

"Oh yes," said the restaurant owner, "I am feeling already like I am with an old friend. Of course, in the Indian story the girl is wearing a red sari, and I'm afraid that the beast is a tiger, but I am always liking this story very much."

"Hmmm," said 2.15, "so if I ever go to India, I shall paint yellow stripes on myself. Meanwhile, dear Lucy, take this menu to Sir Samuel and ask him what he wants."

Lucy took the menu to Sir Samuel and returned with his order. When Mr Al-u-Din saw the long order he stared. "My goodness, look at this!

"1 chicken tikka

1 lamb doupiaza

6 onion bajees

17 poppadums

1 beef korma

2 naans

1 vegetable biriani with curry

3 raitas

4 pillau rice

and lots of mango chutney.

"Oh dear," continued Mr Al-u-Din, "this man is very hungry. You must keep him a prisoner for a long time I am thinking, for a man with such an appetite is very good for business!"

About half an hour later Mr Al-u-Din staggered into the warehouse carrying all the food, and in no time Sir Samuel, Lucy, 2.15 and Mr Al-u-Din were seated in a circle on orange boxes eating curry. Sir Samuel said he'd forgotten how good Indian food was, and 2.15 was delighted to discover a new cuisine. Sir Samuel was so hungry he crammed the food into his mouth.

"Pardon me for wolfing it down," he explained, "but I'm starving."

2.15 stopped eating and looked at Sir Samuel with amazement. "Wolfing? Wolfing? he said with disgust. "Come, sir, what can you mean?"

"You know," replied Sir Samuel, "stuffing it in, eating like a pig."

"Sir," said 2.15, getting up to leave in protest, "I have never been so insulted in my life. May I point out to you that wolves have very elegant table manners. What and who we eat may be a matter of some dispute, but never, sir, I repeat never, do we eat in an unseemly manner."

"It's just a way of putting things, 2.15," said Lucy soothingly. "I don't think Sir Samuel meant to hurt your feelings."

"No indeed," said the surprised Sir Samuel. "Sorry, 2.15."

"Huh," said 2.15. "Well, you watch what you say in future. People say all sorts of things about wolves without thinking."

"Are you finding my food to your taste?" asked Mr Al-u-Din, trying hard to change the subject.

"Dear friend," cried 2.15, "you may not be Aladdin of the Magic Lamp, but you are a cook without compare."

"I am so glad that you are liking my food," said Mr Al-u-Din. "And I regret that I am not Aladdin, for it would be much easier to rub a lamp than to cook all the time, and then I would have enough money to bring Mrs Al-u-Din and my two children over from India and I would not be so lonely."

"How is the business doing?" asked Sir Samuel.

"Not so bad," replied Mr Al-u-Din. "People are just beginning to know me and come back again and again, but when you pull down my restaurant I shall have to begin all over again, and goodness knows when I'll see Mrs Al-u-Din and my children."

"Oh dear," said Sir Samuel. "That sounds bad. But we could have an Indian restaurant in the new complex and that would be very nice. I could lunch there myself."

"I would not be able to afford the rent of an establishment in your complex," said Mr Al-u-Din sadly.

"Oh well," said Sir Samuel, "I can see that we will have to offer special cheap rents to make things easier for the small businessman in the first couple of years."

"Mr Al-u-Din," cried 2.15, "Fate sent you to us. Sir Samuel is coming round to our way of thinking already."

Later Gran and Grandad arrived with a van full of furniture. Grandad stopped in his tracks when he saw Sir Samuel, and Sir Samuel stared back with an amazed look on his face.

"Cor blimey," said Grandad, "if it ain't me old Sergeant-Major, Sam Wolf. 'Allo, Sarge."

"Bert, Bert Wood. Well, blow me down, I hardly recognized you."

"Do you two know each other?" asked Gran.

"Yeah," said Grandad. "This is me old Sergeant-Major, Sam Wolf, known as Soapie Sam."

"Oh, come on, Bert, don't rake all that up," said Sir Samuel quickly.

"Well, Sarge, I certainly am surprised to see you," said Grandad.

"Didn't you recognize the name in all the fuss and bother over my little development?" asked Sir Samuel.

"*Little development*?" snapped Gran. "You're about to change the whole character of this area and you go on about a *little development*? To us, I'll have you know, it's a very big development, and no use to our community as it stands."

"You'd better watch what you say to her, Sarge," said Grandad proudly. "She's my missus and she's organizing the campaign against you."

"It's been hurtful to me, that campaign," complained Sir Samuel. "I'm only a local lad trying to improve the slums I was born in, and all I get is abuse and kidnapping."

"It's what you deserve," said Gran hotly, "smashing up the place and not even bothering to consult the local people whose whole lives will be affected."

"Yes," agreed Grandad. "You never used to be like that – in the army you were a fair and democratic kind of chap, that's why we all liked you."

"Sorry, Bert, sorry, Mrs Wood," said Sir Samuel sheepishly. "I never thought it through, I'm beginning to see that I was wrong."

"Well, about time too," announced Gran. "Now,

come on, we've got to unload the van."

Soon they had a carpet down in a corner of the warehouse, a bed, lots of cushions, a calor gas heater, hurricane lamps, a television, a radio, lots of books and newspapers, a packet of cards, Monopoly, dominoes and Scrabble. Gran went off to make tea with 2.15, and Grandad and Sir Samuel sat down to have a little chat.

"What I don't get, Bert," said Sir Samuel, "is what your connection with this wolf is."

"'Ee just turned up one day, Sarge. My granddaughter, Lucy here, was walkin' through the forest on 'er way to catch the train to London, when this wolf mistakes 'er for bloomin' Red Ridin' 'Ood and 'ee follows 'er out of the forest. Then 'ee can't cope and 'as to pretend to be 'er dog and come to London."

"Couldn't cope? Couldn't cope? Him?" snorted Sir Samuel.

"Oh, 'ee learnt quick enough, Sarge. 'Ee's very clever, that wolf, reads a lot and that. Got fanciful ideas though, that's 'is trouble, wants everyone to live 'appily ever after and all that."

"Ridiculous," proclaimed Sir Samuel loudly.

"That's what I thought," said Grandad, "but you'd be surprised 'ow 'ee manages it."

"Well, you won't see me living happily ever after," declared Sir Samuel, "and that's a promise."

"Famous last words," said Grandad laughing. "Wanna bet on it?"

Gran came back with tea and surveyed the

transformed warehouse. "That lot should keep you comfortable and amused," she said.

"Oh, I'll be snug as a bug in a rug, thanks, Mrs W," said Sir Samuel.

"You can call me Mavis," said Gran. "And I think you're enjoying this kidnapping."

"Don't let on to 2.15," whispered Sir Samuel, "but I am. Meeting old friends and making new ones, and that wolf is quite a character."

"You can say that again," said Gran. "He's the best thing that's happened round here in a long while."

Soon Sir Samuel was sitting on some cushions playing Monopoly with Gran, Grandad, Lucy, 2.15 and Mr Al-u-Din. "Haven't had time to play games for years," he said. "I'm a bit rusty, but I'll beat you lot into a cocked hat."

But he was wrong. Lucy and 2.15 playing together beat him easily.

"Ha," said 2.15, grinning broadly, "I'm beginning to think I'm the one who should be in this property lark!"

Chapter Eight
THE ISLE OF DOGS

That night 2.15 and Sir Samuel took a walk together, and early in the morning they sat by the river and watched the sun come up.

"I haven't had time to watch the sunrise or a sunset for years," mused Sir Samuel wistfully.

"Too busy getting rich?" asked 2.15.

"Just so," answered the millionaire. "Silly, really."

Later, when Lucy arrived with fried-egg sandwiches for their breakfast, she brought a whole batch of morning papers.

"You're certainly making the headlines," Lucy told them.

"Jolly good," said 2.15.

"Yes," agreed Sir Samuel. "And we've got them all bamboozled."

"'*Millionaire vanished without trace*'," read 2.15 from one paper.

"'*Sir Sam's whereabouts a mystery*'," Lucy quoted from another paper.

"Listen to this one," said the millionaire, "'*No ransom demand made, police puzzled*'. Who cares!" cried Sir Samuel. "I haven't had so much fun for years – lots of time, new friends, good food, no responsibilities, this is the life!"

"It says here," remarked 2.15, holding up a

paper to the light, "that your wife is very worried and begs anyone with any information to contact her or the police."

"Humbug," said Sir Samuel gloomily. "It's all show. She doesn't care about me."

"I think you're being very cruel and heartless," said 2.15. "The poor lady is very sad. Come, dear friend, send her a letter saying that you are alive and well."

"No point," replied the millionaire, munching his second fried-egg sandwich.

"Lucy, dear," said 2.15, "would you just slip out and buy me twelve big, fresh, sweet-smelling red roses?" Ten minutes later Lucy returned clutching a huge bunch of roses.

"Oh, flowers now," commented Sir Samuel. "We are getting posh in our warehouse."

"They are not for us," said 2.15, sailing out. "I shall be away for a short while and you are on your Cub's honour not to try to escape."

"Cub's honour then," agreed the millionaire cheerfully, as he sipped away at his tea.

Lucy spent the morning playing cards and Scrabble with Sir Samuel. At lunch time Mr Al-u-Din came over with a curry and they turned on the television news. The newscaster read out, "The first hint that the missing millionaire Sir Samuel Wolf is still alive occurred today when his wife, Beryl, received a bouquet of twelve red roses, purportedly from her husband. The note accompanying the flowers said he was well and thinking of her. The police say the note was not in Sir Samuel's handwriting."

"Oh," said Sir Samuel. "Well, now we know where 2.15 went. Not to worry. Let's play poker now." They left the television on in case there was any more news.

As the day wore on they began to feel a bit worried because 2.15 had not returned. So Mr Al-u-Din went out to buy an evening newspaper. Ten minutes later he burst into the warehouse flourishing the paper.

"Look!" he cried. "Look! Oh dear, this is bad news."

"Give it here," snapped Sir Samuel, snatching it. He read the report out loud.

"The flowers delivered today to Lady Wolf, wife of the missing millionaire, were delivered on a motorbike stolen in the East End of London. Lady Wolf says the delivery man was wearing a helmet and she did not see his face. The man was tall and hairy and had a pleasant manner. The police are now concentrating their search for Sir Samuel on London's East End where Sir Samuel owns considerable amounts of redevelopment land."

"Oh dear," agreed Lucy, "the trail is getting close. But where is 2.15?"

"Haven't got a clue," said Sir Samuel.

"I cannot imagine why 2.15 should not be

back," worried Mr Al-u-Din.

"Let's not panic," said Sir Samuel. "If he's not back tomorrow we'll have to think about hospitals and things."

However, the next morning there was still no sign of 2.15. Gran and Grandad, Sir Samuel, Mr Al-u-Din and Lucy sat round looking miserable.

"We can't just sit here," said Gran firmly. "Now, the first thing to do is to check the Battersea Dogs' Home. Maybe 2.15 got picked up as a stray."

"Good idea," said Sir Samuel. "Here, use this ten pounds to take a taxi."

Gran and Lucy hurried off to the Dogs' Home as fast as they could. When they arrived they gave the man in charge 2.15's description. The man looked through the list for the previous day and said that just such a dog had been picked up in a tube station the day before.

As they went through to get 2.15 the man commented, "Funny-looking dog, isn't he? More like a wolf if it wasn't for the coat."

"Umm," said Lucy. "He's a Great Alaskan Foxhound, you don't get many of them."

"He seemed happy enough here last night," said the man. At that moment they got to the cage where 2.15 was locked in. The man unlocked the cage and 2.15 trotted out. Lucy knelt down and put her arms around him.

"You took your time," 2.15 whispered in her ear. "What kept you?"

"Sorry," she whispered back. "We didn't know where to look."

As they left, 2.15 barked to the other dogs as he passed them. When Gran and Lucy and 2.15 got into the taxi, Gran said, "It sounded like you were saying 'goodbye' to all those dogs."

"I was," said 2.15 cheerfully. "I had a good time, I learnt dog language and now I can talk to wolves and people *and* dogs."

"So it wasn't too bad then?" asked Gran.

"No," answered the wolf. "Food was pretty awful, but otherwise it was fine."

Gran took some crisps out of her bag and 2.15

munched them gratefully. Soon they were back at the warehouse drinking tea and listening to 2.15's experiences.

"A station-master picked me up just after I'd delivered the flowers. I wondered whether I ought to explain the situation to the dear man, but on balance I decided not to."

"I'm glad you showed a bit of sense," grumbled Sir Samuel."

"So I was transported to the Dogs' Home and incarcerated in the cage from which I was later rescued," continued 2.15. "However, never one to waste an opportunity, in that brief time I learnt to bark and thus was able to communicate with my fellow prisoners. Listen," and 2.15 proceeded to bark in various keys. "And so, dear friends, I learnt the stories of all those poor dogs – most affecting – and do you know some of them weren't lost at all? They had run away and don't want their owners to find them. One dog, Rory Retriever from Romford, was never fed. Then there was poor old Willy Whippet from Wanstead – he lived in a flat and never got any exercise. And as for Sally Sealyham from Slough, she got kicked regularly. But I ask you, what will happen when their cruel owners want them back? They'll be handed back with no argument, no discussion, no consideration of what the dogs want. It's not right, it really isn't."

"Oh dear," said Lucy. "It doesn't seem right, it doesn't seem right at all."

"Yes," agreed 2.15, "I know you would look upon it like that, and so I informed them that they would all be rescued tonight."

"Oh yes?" said Grandad. "And 'oo is going to rescue them? That's what I want to know."

"You, of course," replied 2.15, "with a little essential help from me."

"Forget it," snapped Grandad. "You just forget it, mate."

"Oh, Grandad," squeaked Lucy, "all those poor, unhappy dogs."

"I can't go stealin' dogs from the Dogs' Home," said Grandad. "I'm a law-abiding man, or was."

"You helped rescue 3.45 from the zoo," 2.15 reminded him. "Let's ask the lads to help us again. But this time you will all be reunited under the wonderful leadership of the Sarge here."

"Are you saying my old platoon were behind the break-out of a wolf from a zoo?" demanded Sir Samuel.

"Well, yes, Sarge," admitted Grandad.

"Not possible," said Sir Samuel. "You're all old men."

"Not that old, Sarge," said Grandad huffily. "We had a bit of training first and we did a great job. Got 3.45 out of the zoo as easy as one, two, three, and then we got them back to the forest to live 'appily ever after, no trouble."

"Well," gasped Sir Samuel. "There's a thing."

"If they can do it, you can," said 2.15. "What do

you say? Will you command this mission?"

"If you're game, I am," said Sir Samuel. "Now, you go out and get the others on the phone and tell them that the Sarge wants them round here tonight, and that's an order."

So Grandad, grumbling quietly to himself, went off to phone his old mates.

"It's all well and good to go and rescue these dogs," said the millionaire after he'd gone, "but what are you going to do with them afterwards?"

"We could keep them here," suggested 2.15, "and then we could call it the Isle of Dogs."

"But it's already called the Isle of Dogs," commented Sir Samuel.

"Well, then," said 2.15, "we don't have a problem."

Later that day Grandad brought the lads over to the warehouse. To celebrate the reunion Sir Samuel gave Grandad enough money to get in a crate of beer and to buy the best meal ever from Mr Al-u-Din. All the lads were very surprised to see their old Sergeant-Major and even more surprised to discover he was the famous Sir Samuel Wolf. When the meal was over, Sir Samuel got the lads lined up.

"All right, lads," he said. "We're going out on a mission tonight to rescue some dogs."

"Dogs, Sarge?" asked Lew Solomons.

"Yes, dogs!" repeated Sir Samuel. "Dogs in the Battersea Dogs' Home that do not wish to be returned to their owners. Last time you lot went on a mission it was to rescue a wolf, and this time it's to rescue four

dogs. Now, let's see if any of you remember the drill you learnt in the army. All right, you 'orrible bunch of men, line up! Attention! Right turn, quick march!"

So the lads all lined up and 2.15 decided to join in. Mr Al-u-Din said his father had been in the British Army for thirty years and he joined in, too.

For an hour they marched up and down in the warehouse. 2.15 had some trouble keeping up as he wasn't used to using only two legs.

"All right, you 'orrible wolf," yelled the Sarge. "Don't you know your left paw from your right?"

"Enjoying your revenge, Sir Samuel?" asked 2.15.

"Nobody said you had to join in," replied Sir Samuel. "Since you chose to, I shall exploit my position. On the double – left, left, left, left!"

After a while the lads were tired and when they were having a rest Sir Samuel explained his rescue plan to them.

"You'll have to pretend to be the dogs' owners," he told them. "You go in one at a time and say that you're looking for a particular dog. 2.15 will give you all the details. 2.15 will go in with the first one of you and explain to the dogs what is happening. So all you have to do is collect the dogs and bring them back here before anyone realizes that they're not actually your dogs."

"Sarge," groaned Taffy Edwards, "if that's the plan, we didn't need to do all that square-bashing."

"I know," grinned the Sarge, "but I just wanted to see if you were still up to it. And, lads, I'm proud of you. Forty years on and you're still a grand bunch."

Soon all the dogs who wanted to escape were rescued. The others wanted to wait for their owners to find them. 2.15 spent some time trying to persuade a poodle with a very elaborate haircut and bows all over to join them, but she said she liked her haircut and her bows, so eventually 2.15 gave up.

"Do you know," he told Lucy in an incredulous tone, "Mademoiselle Fifi actually *likes* going to the dog parlour and she doesn't mind looking like that one bit. Oh well, nowt so queer as dogs," he commented as they piled into the getaway van and made for the warehouse on the Isle of Dogs.

Chapter Nine
WEREWOLF IN LONDON

When they got back to the warehouse Gran and Lucy had a big supper ready. While everyone tucked in, Sir Samuel and the lads talked a lot about the good old days and agreed that there would be regular reunions from now on, and not just when 2.15 or his friends were in trouble.

"Yes," said Ted Walker, "and as a special concession the Sarge here can come too."

"Oh, thank you," said Sir Samuel sarcastically. "Too kind."

As this discussion was going on, the rescued dogs raced around barking and fighting and generally making a lot of noise. 2.15 barked at them.

"It's no good," he moaned. "They keep forgetting what I tell them. I tell them to be quiet but a moment later they're at it again."

"Well, they can't stay here," said Paddy O'Connor. "That's plain."

"Yes," agreed Lew Solomons. "That number of dogs being noisy would attract attention."

"Can't 'ave that," said Grandad. "Not until the Sarge here gives in about consulting with the Residents' Committee."

One of the dogs barked loudly at 2.15. The wolf nodded. "They want to watch television," he told

Sir Samuel. "They say they'll be quiet if they can watch the advertisements."

So the television was put on. When an advertisement for dog food came on showing a dog gulping down a particular brand of dog food and then barking with satisfaction, the dogs rolled on the floor of the warehouse and howled.

"What's up with them?" asked Grandad.

"It's the advertisement," explained 2.15. "People think the dog is saying that he likes the food, when what he is actually saying is, 'It's awful, I'm only eating it because I'm starving. This brand is the pits, don't let your owners buy it for you'."

"Honestly," said Gran, "We've got to get those dogs out of here. They don't seem to be able to be quiet even watching television. Just as everything is going so nicely, they'll get us into trouble."

So it was agreed that each of the lads should take a dog until a more long-term arrangement could be made. Fred Smith and Bill Andrews were a bit worried that their wives wouldn't like it, but Sir Samuel drew himself up to his full height. "All right, you 'orrible little men," he yelled in his best Sergeant-Major voice, "you take those animals away with you and that's an order. Understand?"

"Yes, Sarge," they replied meekly, and soon they had all departed with the dogs, leaving Sir Samuel and 2.15 alone.

"Why don't you give in and consult the Residents' Committee?" 2.15 asked.

"Not yet," said Sir Samuel. "I'm having far too much fun being kidnapped."

"I'm not sure that kidnapped is the right word," mused 2.15. "Cubnapped would be more like it."

"All right," said Sir Samuel, "I'm having far too much fun being cubnapped to give in."

"Well, if we're going to be together for a bit longer, we ought to get out a bit and go to things," said 2.15.

"Like what?" asked Sir Samuel.

"Like films and concerts and theatres," replied 2.15.

"Dogs can't go to those things," Sir Samuel pointed out.

"No indeed," said 2.15, "but now that I am a master

of disguises, I don't have to be a dog. And you'll have to be disguised too. You can't look like you or you'll be recognized and rescued from the cubnapping."

"Can't have that," agreed Sir Samuel quickly.

It was decided that when they went to the concert 2.15 would be all wrapped up in a wheelchair and Sir Samuel would wear the chauffeur's uniform and a false moustache and big glasses. 2.15 chose a programme of music by Wolfgang Amadeus Mozart, *Wolf Ferrari* and *Hugo Wolf*. "Us wolves are well represented in the music world," he told Sir Samuel.

In the interval Sir Samuel in his uniform wheeled 2.15 into the bar. They both had a drink. In the bar was a beautiful, famous actress. Sir Samuel stared at her and then whistled.

"Stop it!" said 2.15. "You're making me ashamed of you."

"No harm in a little wolf whistle," said Sir Samuel.

"A *what*?" retorted 2.15.

"Oh, dear," groaned Sir Samuel, "now I've offended you. That's what it's called, a wolf whistle."

"Sir," said the outraged wolf, "let me tell you that we wolves show a great respect for women. We may eat them now and again, but we would never, never whistle at them in that vulgar fashion."

In spite of the wolf whistle they both had a splendid time at the concert. Sir Samuel saw lots of people he knew and none of them recognized him. The trip was such a success that their next outing was to a film – *Werewolf of London*. This time Sir Samuel wore dark glasses and carried a white stick and 2.15 pretended to be his guide dog. That evening they went to the pub and 2.15 wore some old clothes and a cloth cap down over his face.

"Me name's Seamus O'Wolf," he told the people in the pub. The next day they went shopping in the market. 2.15 enjoyed the bargaining with the people on the stalls.

"Ma name is Hamish MacWolf," he told the stall owners, "and naebody puts one over on me."

Gran, Grandad and Lucy watched 2.15's capers with some concern.

"2.15 is getting a bit careless," said Grandad. "If 'ee doesn't watch it a bit, 'ee'll get 'is comeuppance."

So Grandad wasn't entirely surprised when one morning a policeman turned up on his doorstep.

"I wonder if I could have a word with you, sir," said the police officer, "on rather an odd matter."

Grandad's heart sank. "'Course," he said. "Come on in."

"Well," began the policeman, "it's a bit hard to explain. Er, yes, well, you see, well, it's like this, sir. We think there's a werewolf round these parts and that maybe you could help us find him."

"A werewolf!" exclaimed Grandad. "Come off it – there's no such thing. Only in horror films and that."

"That's what we all thought, sir," replied the police officer. "But we've come to the conclusion that that is the only explanation for the very odd goings-on around here. We've reluctantly come to the

conclusion that there is a werewolf on these very streets."

"What makes you think that?" asked Grandad.

"Well, you know that werewolves are suppose to be ordinary people during the day and turn into wolves at night – that is, they get very hairy and fierce. Well, this werewolf seems to be the other way round. He is a wolf by day, and maybe turns into a man at night…"

"I see," said Grandad. "Well, I 'ope you don't think it's me."

"Oh no," said the police officer.

"So what's it all about then?" asked Grandad.

"It's like this, sir. First of all a dog steals handbags in Central London, then that French onion seller's clothes were stolen and the miscreant called himself Gaston Loup."

"What of it?" asked Grandad.

"Loup is French for wolf, and so it's Gaston Wolf. Then after that there was Mr de Marco's ice-cream van, and that time the name was Lupo, which is Italian for wolf. Then Sir Samuel Wolf disappears and Mr de Marco gets a cheque for five hundred pounds from Sir Samuel. And most suspicious of all, the letter containing the cheque was posted near here."

"Oh," said Grandad, thinking that 2.15 had not been very careful in covering his tracks.

"Yes," said the policeman, "and every description of the man that we've managed to get says he is very hairy and tries to keep his face covered."

"Very suspicious behaviour," Grandad remarked.

"Oh yes, indeed, sir. Recently it has come to our attention that a man answering the description of Gaston Loup and Giuseppe Lupo has been seen on different occasions round here calling himself Seamus O'Wolf or Hamish MacWolf. Very odd, you must admit."

"Oh, very odd," agreed Grandad. "Very odd indeed."

"What's odd?" asked Gran as she came in carrying a basket full of pamphlets.

"You'll never believe this, love," said Grandad. "The officer 'ere says the police are looking for a werewolf."

"A what?" asked Gran.

"You may wonder, madam," said the policeman. "But the only way we can make any sense of this wolf business is that there is a werewolf roaming these streets, part-man, part-wolf. Now I know it sounds silly, but we're asking everyone – do you have any information that might lead to the apprehension of this werewolf?"

"Officer," said Gran, smiling, "I can honestly say I don't know anything about a werewolf. Now, take one of these pamphlets – it's about the redevelopment scheme."

"Oh yes," said the policeman, putting on his helmet. "I live round here, you know. I'll come to the big meeting tomorrow night."

"Good," said Gran. "See you then. Keep looking for the werewolf."

"We'd better get round to the warehouse," said Gran the moment the policeman had left, "and tell them what's happening. 2.15 had better let Sir Sam go and then we should take 2.15 back to the forest as soon as possible – out of harm's way. It's all getting a bit out of hand."

"You can say that again," said her husband. "Come on."

When they arrived at the warehouse, 2.15 and Sir Samuel were glued to the television.

"Hello," said Grandad.

"Hello," said Gran. "We've got important news."

"Sssh," said Sir Samuel.

"Sssh," said 2.15.

Gran and Grandad looked at the television. On the screen was a woman in tears.

"My wife," said Sir Samuel. They all looked at the television screen.

"So I say to the person who kidnapped my husband, please let him come home, he is much missed," the woman sobbed.

"She loves me!" shrieked Sir Samuel. "She really loves me – not the money, me! Hurray!" And he grabbed Gran and began dancing.

"I want to go home, I agree to consult anyone and everyone but I want to get home to my own dear Beryl."

"Listen!" said Grandad. "Come on, you two, stop

dancin' around like young things. We've got somethin' to tell you."

"What, pray?" asked 2.15.

"That the police are lookin' for a werewolf. They've rumbled Gaston Loup and Guiseppe Lupo, and they're looking for a man who turns into a wolf by day."

"Oh well," said 2.15, "I don't look much like a wolf these days, so I'm not worried."

"Well, to be on the safe side," said Gran, "we think you should go home."

"Home?" cried 2.15. "Back to my own dear 3.45? Yes, I shall go home to my loved one, now I have made sure that the community will live happily ever after."

"Quiet," said Grandad. "Look, there's a special bulletin. Let's listen." They all fell silent and listened intently to the TV.

"The police say they have made an arrest in connection with the 'Wolfman' crimes that have been bedevilling the East End of London," said the reporter.

"Oh dear," said 2.15. "Who can it be?"

Just then, Lucy burst into the warehouse. "2.15, come quickly, something terrible has happened! The police have arrested 3.45!"

There was a moment's silence.

"Arrested 3.45!" exclaimed 2.15. "That's not possible. She's safe in the forest."

"She's not, 2.15!" said Lucy urgently. "I saw this

wolf that looked like 3.45 in the playground outside the flats. I was just going down to get her when the police drove up in a van and grabbed her."

"It may not have been her," said Sir Samuel.

"It was," insisted Lucy. "She said, 'Find 2.15!' before they locked her in the van and drove off. 2.15, you've got to do something! You know how 3.45 feels about people. If they lock her up for any length of time it will be awful. She'll eat someone for sure if she's kept behind bars again. It will remind her of the zoo!"

"It's all out of 'and," said Grandad. "I said it would be and it is – completely out of 'and!"

Chapter Ten

All's Well That Ends Well

When 2.15 heard the news about 3.45 he raced for the door shouting out, "Quick, come on, not a moment to be lost. My beloved is being held against her will."

Long before Grandad or Gran or Sir Samuel could catch up with him, 2.15 burst through the doors of the police station. "Unlock my dear one," he proclaimed to the amazed officer on duty. "I'm the one you want."

"Excuse me, sir," replied the bamboozled policeman, "but what do you mean?"

"My wife, 3.45 – you're holding her in the cell. But it's me you want really."

"You?"

"Yes," said 2.15 patiently. "You arrested her thinking she was me, but she's not. I'm me, she's her."

"And who are you?" asked the policeman.

"I'm the dangerous werewolf you've been looking for."

"Put that man, I mean that wolf, in a cell," yelled the police officer.

"As you wish," said 2.15, holding out his front paws to be put into handcuffs. At that moment Gran, Grandad, Lucy and Sir Samuel burst in.

"Don't worry," 2.15 told them, "I've explained to

this officer that I'm me and that 3.45 isn't me, she's her, and he understands everything."

"I don't, I don't," groaned the police officer. "I don't understand anything. I'm confused, totally confused."

"It's all very simple really," said 2.15. "Now what happened was this…" and he told the policeman everything from the beginning; when he followed Lucy out of the forest thinking she was Red Riding Hood and caught the 2.15 to London. After a while the policeman stopped taking notes and just stared at 2.15 in amazement.

"And so," finished 2.15 with a flourish, "I finally persuaded Sir Samuel to consult with the good people of this area, so please, sir, be so kind as to release my wife who has committed no crimes at all."

"Well," muttered the policeman, "I never heard the like before, never in all my born days."

"It's all true, mate," Grandad reassured him. "Every blinkin' word is true."

"Yes," said Lucy, "and now that he's confessed, I think you should let 3.45 go."

"Can't do that, miss," said the policeman. "She escaped from the zoo. She'll have to go back."

"Oh no!" cried Gran, Lucy and Grandad.

"All right, everyone, calm down," said Sir Samuel. "I'll deal with this. Now listen, officer, I'm not going to bring any charges against 2.15, he did me a great favour and this community a great service, so I think you would have a problem making a charge stick."

"You mean he kidnapped you and you don't mind?" asked the amazed policeman.

"Kidnapped?" replied Sir Samuel. "Who was kidnapped? No, I just decided to take a little holiday with my good friend 2.15 here."

"A holiday! What, in a warehouse?"

"Well, why not?" asked Sir Samuel. "After all, it is *my* warehouse."

"That's all well and good," complained the policeman, "but half the police in London have been looking for you, and your wife has been very upset."

"It was very remiss of me not to have informed the authorities and my dear wife of my sudden decision, but I just felt a great need to get away from it all. I was overworked and not myself and I was under my Cub's honour."

"You were what?"

"Oh, forget it," said Sir Samuel hurriedly. "Nothing, nothing."

"Well," said the policeman, "what a can of worms. I think I'll have to lock up all of you in the cells while I call my superiors in on the case. I don't know what to make of all this."

So a handcuffed 2.15 and Sir Samuel, Gran, Grandad and Lucy all traipsed off to the cells.

"You certainly took your time," snapped 3.45 as they crowded into the cell.

"My love, my love," said 2.15, kissing her paw. "Please meet my friend, Sir Samuel Wolf."

"Any friend of yours is not a friend of mine," said

3.45 and she sat with her back to all of them.

"Hello, 3.45," said Lucy tentatively. "You remember me?"

"I most certainly do," said the wolf. "You promised me he wouldn't get into trouble, and now look where we are."

"2.15 didn't do anything bad," said Grandad. "Well, he did, but not that bad. He was only trying to help."

"Help who?" sniffed 3.45. "People, I suppose."

"Well, yes," said Gran. 'Anything wrong with that?"

"A waste of time, people," sniffed 3.45. "A complete and utter waste of time."

"My dear good woman," began Sir Samuel. 3.45 shot him a fierce glare.

"Er, umm, I mean my dear good wolf. Your husband has played a very positive role in this community, and indeed in my life, since he reunited me with my wife."

"Has he indeed?" sniffed 3.45. "Well, that was very nice of him, since he can't be bothered with his own wife."

"It's true," cried 2.15. "I have neglected you, my love, but not for want of caring. You do not have a postal address or a telephone number."

"You could have written to Lucy's mum," cried 3.45. "She's all right as people go. She'd have come into the forest and found me."

"Yes," agreed Lucy. "Or you could have phoned

Mum and left a message. I think you're really rotten to just abandon poor 3.45 like that."

2.15 hung his head in shame, while Gran took up the refrain.

"That just wasn't right, 2.15, neglecting your wife like that. I wouldn't like it one bit if Grandad did that to me!"

"A bit off," agreed Sir Samuel, "though maybe people who live in glass houses shouldn't throw stones."

"I'm surprised at you, 2.15, being so unkind," continued Lucy. "*And* thoughtless and inconsiderate."

"Yeah," chipped in Grandad. "I mean, charity begins at 'ome and all that."

"I'm an utter cad," said 2.15 shamefacedly. "A cad and a bounder. My dear, can you ever forgive me?"

3.45 looked at him and sniffed. "Have to, I suppose," she said, "since I'm going to have cubs."

"Cubs!" yelled 2.15. "Did you hear that? Cubs! I'm going to be a father. Hurray!"

"That's why I came to London to find you," explained 3.45.

"My love, my love," said 2.15 fondly, and he put his handcuffed paws round her and gave her a kiss. The others all crowded around giving congratulations. In the middle of it all the policeman came back.

"All right, all right," said the policeman, "quieten down, you lot."

"Congratulate me, officer. I'm going to be a father!" cried 2.15.

"Oh, that is good news," said the policeman, holding out his hand to congratulate 2.15. Realizing that 2.15 was handcuffed, he patted him on the back instead.

"Thank you," said 2.15. "Now, officer, I'm sure you'll agree that this is no place for an expectant mother. What are you going to do about it?"

"It's out of my hands now," explained the policeman. "I rang the Chief and told him what was going on…"

"And?" asked 2.15.

"He thought I'd gone mad, and he's coming over in person to sort out what's happened."

In the distance they could hear the howling of

police sirens. The sirens got nearer and soon the Commissioner of the Metropolitan Police was racing down the stairs to the cells.

"All right, officer," he snapped. "Now what's all this nonsense about you holding the wolf from *Red Riding Hood* in handcuffs?"

"Good day, sir," called 2.15, holding up his manacled paws. "It is I to whom the good officer referred in your earlier conversation."

"Well, I'll be blowed," said the Chief of Police. "The wolf really can talk. I don't know what to make of this at all! Will someone please tell me the story from the beginning?"

So 2.15 told the story, with frequent interruptions from the others. When he had finished, the Commissioner of the Metropolitan Police looked as bewildered as the rest of the police force.

"Well," he exclaimed. "My goodness me! I never heard anything like it. I don't know what to do. I suppose I'd better phone the Home Secretary."

So he phoned the Home Secretary, who didn't know what to do either and said to phone the Prime Minister. So they phoned the Prime Minister who was amazed and didn't know what to do either and said to phone the Queen. So the Head of the Metropolitan Police phoned the Queen, who thought it was all wonderful and wanted to speak to 2.15 himself. 2.15 was allowed out of his cell and had the handcuffs taken off, then he picked up the phone.

"Good evening, ma'am," he said. "Oh, how nice of

you to say that. Oh, thank you very much. Yes, indeed, ma'am, I shall pass the message on. So kind, thank you. Goodbye."

"Well?" said the Commissioner of the Metropolitan Police. "What did she have to say?"

"She said that she had always loved the story of *Red Riding Hood* and so did her children and grandchildren, and she regarded me as an old friend, and I'm to be released immediately and so is 3.45. She's going to tell you that herself. Come, sir, take the phone and talk to your monarch."

"There," said Sir Samuel. "All's well that ends well."

"Huh," replied 3.45. "It very nearly *didn't* all end well."

"Well, I couldn't have known that the Queen was an old friend of yours," complained the Commissioner of the Metropolitan Police.

"Oh, she's not," 2.15 assured him. "I've never met the Queen, but I'm an old friend of hers from her childhood."

"Under the circumstances, I think you two wolves should leave this town as soon as possible," said the Commissioner of the Metropolitan Police.

"Yes," agreed Sir Samuel, "but not until after the meeting tomorrow of the Residents' Action Committee."

When tomorrow came the meeting of the Residents' Action Committee was packed to the seams. News that Sir Samuel had agreed to talk had spread and the whole neighbourhood wanted to hear what he had to say. On the platform were Sir Samuel and his wife, Gran and Grandad, the rest of the Committee, and 2.15 and 3.45, who were guests of honour. Sir Samuel rose to speak.

"Friends," began Sir Samuel. "I have come here tonight to tell you that I am happy to co-operate with your Committee. As many of you know, I'm a local lad, and in the last few days I've been making contact with my roots and I realize that the people who live round here are the salt of the earth and that nothing is too good for them. So I plan to move down here with my wonderful wife. Also, I have decided to include in my scheme a youth club, a centre for senior citizens, housing, a swimming pool and leisure centre and lots of restaurants with a variety of exciting foods, Greek, Chinese, Indian and a lot more. And I want everyone to know that my door is always open. If anyone thinks I'm doing anything wrong or stupid, come in and say. I'm always willing to listen and learn."

Everyone cheered. Sir Samuel held his hands up for quiet.

"And lastly, I want to thank all my friends of the last few days, but most of all 2.15, who helped me see the error of my ways and that people mean more than money."

Everyone cheered again and called for 2.15.

2.15 stood up and went to the microphone.

"Dear friends," he began, "it makes me feel very happy that everything has worked out so well and that you are going to get the centre you all need and deserve. Still, I can't always be here when things go wrong for people, so people had better work out a different way of going about things because my wife and I off back to the forest to get on with being happy."

After the meeting Sir Samuel gave a huge party in the warehouse. Mr Al-u-Din provided the most delicious food and everyone ate and drank well into the night. As it got near to midnight 2.15 said he and 3.45 had to leave the ball on the stroke of midnight and that he wanted a few words.

"Dear friends," he said, "unaccustomed as I am to public speaking, we would like to thank you for all your good wishes. We hope that you all live happily ever after and I, for one, can see no reason why you shouldn't. Sir Samuel is reunited with Lady Wolf. Gran and Grandad are moving to the forest and the community is saved. Mr Al-u-Din can afford to bring Mrs Al-u-Din and the little Al-u-Dins to London, and the rescued dogs are all happy living with the lads. So goodbye, everyone. Goodbye! Be happy!" And he and 3.45 raced out into the night and, laughing and dancing, set off for the forest.